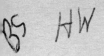

"You Can't Stay Here,"

Elizabeth said in a loud whisper.

Somewhere inside Roberto, a spark of mischief flamed to life. Looking pained, he said, "Can it be that you are ashamed of a humble gondolier, *signorina*?"

"Of course not . . ."

"*Mia d'oro,*" Roberto proclaimed loudly, "I had to see you. I cannot eat, I cannot sleep. Tell me you have not forgotten our night of *grande passione*."

"Last night was a mistake. It was, it was—" Despite the idiotic melodrama he was enacting, she found herself irresistibly drawn to the gondolier, and to his remarkable gray eyes. "What happened last night was . . . not the sort of thing I usually do."

"I would be very happy to change that, my love," he told her in a devastating purr.

Dear Reader:

Series and Spin-offs! Connecting characters and intriguing interconnections to make your head whirl.

In Joan Hohl's successful trilogy for Silhouette Desire— *Texas Gold* (7/86), *California Copper* (10/86), *Nevada Silver* (1/87)—Joan created a cast of characters that just wouldn't quit. You figure out how *Lady Ice* (5/87) connects. And in August, "J.B." demanded his own story—*One Tough Hombre*. In *Falcon's Flight*, coming in November, you'll learn *all* about . . .?

Annette Broadrick's *Return to Yesterday* (6/87) introduced Adam St. Clair. This August *Adam's Story* tells about the woman who saves his life—and teaches him a thing or two about love!

The six Branigan brothers appeared in Leslie Davis Guccione's *Bittersweet Harvest* (10/86) and *Still Waters* (5/87). September brings *Something in Common*, where the eldest of the strapping Irishmen finds love in unexpected places.

Midnight Rambler by Linda Barlow is in October—a special Halloween surprise, and totally unconnected to anything.

Keep an eye out for other Silhouette Desire favorites— Diana Palmer, Dixie Browning, Ann Major and Elizabeth Lowell, to name a few. You never know when secondary characters will insist on their own story. . . .

All the best,

Isabel Swift
Senior Editor & Editorial Coordinator
Silhouette Books

ERIN ROSS
Carnival Madness

Silhouette Desire

Published by Silhouette Books New York

America's Publisher of Contemporary Romance

SILHOUETTE BOOKS
300 East 42nd St., New York, N.Y. 10017

ISBN: 0-373-05383-5

First Silhouette Books printing October 1987

America's Publisher of Contemporary Romance

Printed in the U.S.A.

Books by Erin Ross

Silhouette Special Edition

Flower of the Orient #107

Silhouette Desire

Second Harvest #18
Time for Tomorrow #89
Fragrant Harbor #114
Tide's End #137
Odds Against #155
Child of My Heart #171
Roses for Remembering #217
Willing Spirit #280
Carnival Madness #383

ERIN ROSS

has pursued a wide variety of activities during her life. At one time or another this author studied radio, taught guitar, practiced karate and sang with a rock group. But writing has always been a favorite pursuit. "I'm an avid reader," she explains, "and I think sooner or later all avid readers get the bug to write!"

To my editor, Lucia Macro, for being such a good friend and for taking my best work and making it even better.

And to Marina Russo, in fond memory of an idyllic day spent skiing in the Alps.

With very special thanks to Joanne Navarini, for a fun evening in Turino and for correcting my deplorable Italian.

One

Aunt Celia was late. Again!

Elizabeth Bradshaw first tried to evenly distribute her one hundred and fifteen pounds on the rickety Tudor chair. Then she settled down to nurse her indignation.

It's really too much, she thought, eyeing her watch with mounting impatience. Celia Randolph should be more considerate. Just because the woman was beautiful, charming and filthy rich did not give her the license to forget that some people worked for a living. And this working person could have spent the last sixty-five minutes in more profitable pursuits than cooling her heels in a fifteenth-century English tearoom—no matter how quaint it might be.

Elizabeth re-shifted her weight on the chair and was rewarded by a dangerously loud creak. "Good grief," she moaned, half-aloud. It was one thing to aim for authenticity but enough was enough. She gazed at the low black-beamed ceiling, the small hand-blown panes of glass set into the windows and doors, and the fine old pewter collection and decided the proprietors had done a good job of preserving the old cottage's original flavor. But they might have made an exception in the case of the chairs. When one had a date with the perpetually late Celia Billingsford Randolph, there was a lot to be said for twentieth-century comfort.

Bored, Elizabeth picked up a discarded copy of the *London Informer* someone had left on a nearby chair. The front page of the tabloid blazed with its usual sensational headlines: who had been seen with whom, where and behind whose back?

Today's lead story dealt with a man Elizabeth had heard more than enough of since her arrival in Britain three weeks ago. Roberto Roselli, the famous—or in Elizabeth's opinion—*infamous* Italian playboy. She was tired of reading about the parties he attended, his fabulous stable of horses, his success on the racetrack, his latest romantic conquests. As crown prince of Europe's jet set, Roselli's cocky, too handsome smile had loomed out at her for the past three weeks from nearly every London paper except the *Financial Times*. According to Aunt Celia—and if she didn't know, nobody did—Mr. Roselli was the most eligible bachelor on the continental scene. From the number of gorgeous young women pictured clinging to him both in and out of the winner's circle, he was obviously enjoying his reign.

The photograph accompanying today's story pictured Roselli at a party hosted by a middle-aged couple well-known to London society. His arms were draped around two beautiful women, a blonde and a redhead, both wearing low-cut dresses and inviting expressions. Ugh! Elizabeth thought. They look like lovesick calves!

"Ah-hah! Caught in the act."

At the sound of the familiar contralto voice Elizabeth dropped the paper as if it had suddenly caught fire. "You're late, Celia," she said, scooting the *Informer* under her seat.

Ignoring her niece's censoring tone, Celia Randolph smiled regally at the heads that had turned at her entrance and slipped gracefully into an ancient chair. Elizabeth noted with annoyance that it did not creak.

After placing an order for two curded-cream teacakes—the house specialty consisting of hot scones served with rich, freshly beaten butter—Celia settled back and regarded her niece from beneath a wide-brim purple beaver hat trimmed with pheasant feathers. Elizabeth, along with most of the other patrons, stared at the hat in fascination. It was outrageous.

Then, everything about Celia was outrageous. From her cap of shiny, blue-black hair, dramatically highlighted by a single streak of silver, to her too-perceptive emerald-green eyes and theatrical makeup, Celia Randolph was one of a kind. Elizabeth's aunt also wore a green velvet suit with a vivid scarlet satin blouse and enormous antique Spanish-gold earrings. Only Aunt Celia could get away with that outfit, Elizabeth decided, and contrive to look perfectly marvelous in the process!

"Don't bother to hide it," Celia went on in the voice Elizabeth always thought belonged on the stage. "I saw you poring over that nasty little scandal sheet. What juicy tidbits does the *Informer* have to offer today?"

"Somebody left it on a chair," Elizabeth told her, pouring tea into dainty Wedgwood cups. She added a splash of hot water and a lemon wedge to hers and two cubes of sugar and a healthy measure of cream to her aunt's. "It helped pass the time while I waited for you."

"Time." Celia made a dismissive gesture with her elegantly jeweled hand as if the word did not exist in her vocabulary. "That's one of your problems, Elizabeth, you're always in a rush.'' With a dramatic flick of one long, painted finger, Celia touched a spring on her bracelet watch. "I promised to meet you at three o'clock and that's exactly... oh, dear, it's after four. Where has the day gone?" She smiled disarmingly. "I'm afraid I made rather a late night of it at the Leadbetters' party yesterday."

"The Leadbetters," Elizabeth repeated, wondering why the name seemed familiar. It took a moment before she realized she had just read it in today's *Informer*. That Italian playboy had been at the Leadbetters', along with most of London society. She might have known Celia would be there, too. "I could have used this time at Avebury," she said a bit resentfully. "I leave Saturday for Inverary, Scotland, and I won't have time to go back."

"Avebury!" Celia's tone was disdainful. "It escapes me why anyone would want to bother with a collection of ancient stones. They may be older than Stonehenge but they're frightfully dreary. Surely this romance author of yours isn't going to put the Avebury stones in her book?"

Elizabeth looked sheepish. "No, they won't be included in the novel. Actually she's setting the book here, in Lacock. But since I'm doing a historical article on megalithic monuments—"

"You thought you'd pop over and have a look." Celia shook her head, blithely unaware that the movement set a rain of feathers floating off her hat. "This author—oh, bother, what is her name anyway?"

"Amore. Venus Amore."

"Good Lord!"

"She writes historical romances, Celia."

"I know. But still that's a bit much, isn't it, dear?" Celia took a sip of her tea. "I suppose she's terribly successful at it."

"Terribly. Four best-sellers in a row."

"Gracious. Fancy that." Celia peered out the window at the small village of Lacock, Wiltshire, with its twisting streets and half-timbered, gray-stone facade so reminiscent of fifteenth to eighteenth-century England. The afternoon was turning dark quickly, and a February drizzle lent a dismal cast to the town. Still, Lacock exuded a charm that refused to be daunted by the gloom. "It isn't London, of course," Celia conceded. "But I suppose it *is* pleasant enough in its own way."

"Pleasant enough for Miss Amore to set the first half of her novel here," her niece answered dryly.

Celia looked out again, doubtfully. "I can't imagine why. This seems like one of those awful little villages that rolls up its streets at nine every night. Although I suppose a romance author might make good use of that," Celia added with a wicked grin.

"What Miss Amore does with the information I provide is no business of mine," her niece said primly.

"Don't play coy with me, Elizabeth Bradshaw. You've been researching those books since college. You must know more about the morality, or *immorality*, of eighteenth century Europe than Casanova himself."

"Miss Amore pays very well. And the travel enables me to carry out my own research at the same time."

"For those dreary little historical pieces you write yourself."

"History is my field, Celia."

"Yes, God help us." She regarded her niece frankly over her tea. "So what you'd like me to believe is that you never sneak even a tiny peek at Miss Amore's books."

Elizabeth looked uncomfortable. "Well, of course I have to read them for—"

"Ah-hah!" Celia pounced triumphantly. "I rest my case."

"I was going to say that it's necessary to check them for accuracy. You've got a dirty mind, Celia."

"Nonsense, I have an eminently practical mind. And I find it difficult to believe that a healthy young woman like yourself finds romance so distasteful." Her eyes narrowed. "I suppose what's-his-name, your librarian fiancé, agrees with this research nonsense?"

"His name is Sherman Hamm. And we're not precisely engaged. We have an understanding."

"*Hamm?* My dear, how can you?" Celia looked genuinely alarmed.

"Celia, I've known Sherman since high school. He's an intelligent, sensitive man."

"Whose views are equally unromantic?"

"Sherman places a high value on the intellectual aspects of our relationship, just as I do. We share a great deal in common."

"Intellectual aspects? Good Lord, Elizabeth, you make it sound as if you're contemplating a corporate merger instead of a marriage." She shook her head expressively and several more feathers floated gently into her tea. "What about excitement and passion? Tell me, dear, is there any *fire* between you?"

"You sound like Miss Amore. Fire may sell books, but in real life it's greatly overrated. Look at your sister. This passion of yours has led Mother into three disastrous marriages, with husband number four circling about her house like a vulture. And Dad may be one marriage behind her, but from the sound of his last letter he'll soon be catching up."

Celia used the tip of one long, polished nail to remove the feathers from her tea. "Darling, I do believe you're turning into a cynic."

"I'm just being realistic. I've thought my future out very carefully. It's mutual interests that makes for a long-lasting relationship."

"Well, you're certainly going to have that. The kind of marriage you've described will make one year seem like an eternity."

Celia reached across the table and took her niece's hand. She smiled into the deep-blue eyes that were always too serious even when Elizabeth was a child. The child really was quite attractive with her smooth oval face, generous mouth, stubborn chin, and a thick mass of chestnut hair that defied all Elizabeth's efforts at control. Was it possible this silly girl was unaware of her own appeal? Celia pondered. After all, she was twenty-five, surely she couldn't be such an innocent. Still, one had to wonder. She shuddered at her niece's drab pantsuit and sensible walking shoes. Granted the child had just finished sloshing about looking at old stones, but even that sort of activity could be managed attractively.

"Darling, I agree that companionability is important, but without the excitement, that special chemistry between a man and a woman, you're cheating yourself."

"That's easy for you to say, Celia," Elizabeth said, thinking of her aunt's long, happy marriage. In 1944, as a young army nurse stationed in England during the last days of the Second World War, Celia had met, nursed back to health and after a whirlwind courtship, married Royal Air Force Major George Randolph. Five years ago, after thirty-seven years of wedded bliss, George had died suddenly while on safari with Celia in the Sudan. Determined to preserve her husband's ancestral estates and fortune, Celia continued to make their London residence her home.

"The sort of relationship you had with George is an unrealistic expectation in today's world," Elizabeth added.

"Nonsense. If you put forth any effort at all you could have men eating out of your hand."

"I have absolutely no desire to have men eating out of my hand."

"That's because you've never tried it. It can be very nice, I promise you." Celia considered her niece thoughtfully as she poured out the last of the tea. Having been blessed with no children of her own she had always been close to her only sister's child. The girl had far too much promise to settle for mediocrity. No, it just wouldn't do. Clearly, Elizabeth needed help. "Darling, did you know it's Carnival time in Venice?"

"Venice?" Elizabeth repeated. "You mean Venice, Italy? How did we get on to that?"

"We were speaking of it last night—at the Leadbetters. Have you ever been to Venice during Carnival?"

"I've never been to Venice, period."

"Hmm."

"Celia, you've got that gleam in your eye. What are you up to?"

"Darling, I'm not up to anything. But it's impossible to speak of romance and not think of the most romantic city in the world." She spread her long hands expressively. "During *Carnevale*, as the Venetians say, Venice is incomparable, like life through the looking glass. It's glorious."

"That's nice, Celia. But I don't see—"

"That's just the point, dear. You haven't seen. And you really must see something besides prehistoric rocks and stuffy English villages." She beamed. "That settles it then. We'll spend the last week of your trip in Venice."

"That's impossible. I'm leaving for Scotland on Saturday."

Celia gave a small shudder. "Believe me, dear, you don't want to spend February in Inverary. Dreadful weather."

"But the second half of Miss Amore's book is set there."

"From Lacock to Inverary." Celia clucked sympathetically. "That certainly should try her writing skills." She finished her tea and picked up a pair of purple, rhinestone-studded gloves. "Trust me, darling, you'll be much happier attending Carnival in Venice than snowshoeing around Inverary. I'll have your tickets changed immediately."

"But I don't want my tickets changed." Elizabeth's voice had risen considerably and she looked about the quiet tearoom in embarrassment. In lower tones she continued, "I'm not going to Venice with you."

"Nonsense, dear, of course you are. Everyone will be there, even Rober—er, some people I'm sure you'd like to meet." Celia tilted her head coyly. "You owe it to yourself to have one last fling before you settle down with this—this Hamm person."

"I don't want to have a fling. I'm perfectly happy with my life just the way it is."

Ignoring her niece's objections, Celia paid the bill and rose. "We'll leave on Saturday. That will give me time to take care of one or two things in London, and for you to finish wading about the countryside."

Elizabeth grabbed her things and followed her aunt to the door. "Celia, it's out of the question. I'm not going with you."

Carmichael, Celia's elderly chauffeur, was waiting outside in what had become a pouring rain. Holding up a large umbrella, he escorted his mistress into an ancient Rolls Royce. Before Elizabeth could reach the car, the passenger door had been closed and Carmichael was settling into the driver's seat.

"I'm not going, Celia," Elizabeth shouted, shivering as cold rain ran down her neck. She rapped sharply on the car window while struggling into her coat.

Smiling serenely, Celia blew her niece a kiss. "See you on Saturday," she mouthed, waving brightly as the Rolls pulled away from the curb.

Elizabeth broke into a run behind the limousine. "Will you listen to me? I'm not going with you!"

She sloshed into a puddle and stopped, shaking her fist in frustration at the retreating car. "Dammit, Celia Randolph, this is one time you are not going to get your way. I am not going to go to Venice. And that's final!"

At least it wasn't raining.

This was Elizabeth's first thought as their train pulled into Santa Lucia station early Saturday afternoon. Venice, on this crisp mid-February afternoon, was bathed in sunshine. After three weeks of almost constant rain in England, Elizabeth was at least grateful for that small favor.

With the confidence of a native, Celia supervised the loading of their luggage onto the water taxi that would take them to their hotel. As they sailed effortlessly along the Grand Canal, Elizabeth felt some of her resentment toward Celia abate. Although she abhorred her aunt's strong-arm tactics, Venice really was unique. She felt as if she'd stepped into another world. She was surrounded by a profusion of Byzantine splendor no student of history could resist: palaces, churches, picturesque houses, a seemingly endless series of graceful bridges and smaller canals or *rii*, branching off the main waterway. This was a fairy-tale city, hardly changed since the days of Titian and Tintoretto.

Elizabeth was not surprised to find that her aunt had chosen the best hotel Venice had to offer. Celia Randolph traveled in style and even during Carnival, when the humblest *pensione* was solidly booked, she somehow managed not to compromise her high standards.

Their suite consisted of two bedrooms connected by a common sitting room all overlooking the Canale di San

Marco. Across the lagoon was a breathtaking view of the isle of San Giorgio Maggiore, dominated by Palladio's magnificent sixteenth-century basilica. To the west, Elizabeth could look down on Piazza San Marco, St. Mark's Square, and the Ducal Palace. Carnival revelers were everywhere, thronging through the narrow streets and filtering over slim bridges to explode into the huge piazza below, where a large crowd was watching a troupe of red-suited acrobats perform in painted face. An aura of magical fantasy lay over the city.

"Well, what do you think?" Celia asked, joining her niece at the window. "I told you it had to be seen to be believed."

"I'm seeing it and still I find it difficult to believe."

"Wait until the party tonight. That's when Carnival truly comes to life."

Elizabeth turned to her in surprise. "You didn't say anything about a party."

"Darling, Carnival in Venice *is* a party. One long, lovely party lasting ten days and nights."

"But I—I don't go to parties. I admit the costumes and the performers are interesting, but I have no intention of joining them."

"That's another of your problems, Elizabeth. You watch from the sidelines while life passes you by."

"That's your opinion, Celia," her niece answered testily. "Besides, it's a moot point. I have nothing to wear that would be appropriate."

Elizabeth's heart sank at the twinkle that lit her aunt's eyes. "Of course you do. That was part of my last-minute business in London." She looked her niece over with a practiced eye. "I'm sure you're just about Phyllis Rander's daughter's size."

"Celia, you're doing it again. What does Phyllis Rander's daughter have to do with me?"

With a secret smile, Celia swept off to her bedroom and returned carrying a gorgeous gold-brocaded silk dress over her arm. "Phyllis's daughter went to the Regency Masked Ball two seasons ago as Marie Antoinette. She has graciously loaned you her costume."

Elizabeth stared openmouthed at the gown. "I'm not dressing up in that thing."

"Nonsense. You'll be beautiful, trust me."

"That's what you said when you lured me to Venice. As a spectator. A *spectator*, Celia."

"Elizabeth Bradshaw, you are the most stubborn young woman I have ever met. Of course you will dress up and of course you will attend the party. No one comes to Venice during Carnival without joining in the fun."

"I do, Celia. That's precisely what I do. I observe and I take notes—that's my profession. I do not dress up as Marie Antoinette. And I most certainly do not attend society parties, even in Venice, so you might just as well get that gleam out of your eye. This is one time you are not going to get your way!"

When was she ever going to learn? Elizabeth eyed herself unhappily in the full-length mirror thinking she looked like an overdone puffed pastry. She couldn't remember the last time she'd won an argument with Celia. Why did she even try?

She turned and viewed herself from the rear. There was no denying that the dress was exquisite. Made from Italian silk, brocaded in gold with a delicate rose-and-white floral pattern, it was easily the most beautiful gown Elizabeth had ever seen. It was also cut entirely too low in the front and cinched so tightly at the waist that she found it difficult to breathe. Fine Venetian lace trimmed the bodice and the many layers of sleeve that fell gracefully from mid-arm. To Elizabeth's dismay, Phyllis Rander's daughter had been authentic in other aspects as well, and the wide, stiff hoop Celia had fastened over her slender hips itched and bobbed about disconcertingly when she moved.

"Celia, I'm popping out on top," she said, staring down in alarm at her plunging neckline. "Can't we stick in a piece of lace or something?"

"Darling, you have a perfectly marvelous figure. Don't be afraid to let it show."

"I have on perfectly lovely underwear, too, but I'm darned if I'll let it show."

"Don't be silly, Elizabeth. Nothing makes a woman feel more feminine than sexy undergarments." She fussed a moment with her niece's skirts, then winked at her in the mirror. "And there's nothing more exciting than allowing the right man to discover them."

Elizabeth shook her head. "Celia, you're hopeless."

"Not at all. I'm simply not afraid to advertise the fact that I'm a woman. And you wouldn't either if, just once in your life, you'd relax and see how nice it can be."

When Celia finished with the dress, Elizabeth examined herself critically in the mirror. The gown billowed out from a tightly cinched waist and over a wide hoop into seemingly endless folds of material. "How am I supposed to sit down in this thing?"

"You're not, you're supposed to dance. Now hold still." Celia made one or two final adjustments in her niece's hair, which was styled with a high profusion of curls, powder and cleverly arranged jewels, then stood back to observe the overall effect of her handiwork. "See? I told you. Absolutely stunning."

"I'm wobbly, Celia. You've piled my hair so high I can hardly hold up my head, and these skirts move about so much it makes me dizzy." She took a few hesitant steps to test her mobility then came to an unhappy stop. "It's not going to work. This dress is walking me, not the other way around. What if I fall on my face?"

"Elizabeth, stop complaining. All you need is a little practice. Here, watch me." With a regal tilt of her own powdered head, Celia seemed to float across the room; the elaborate skirts of her Marquise de Pompadour costume gliding easily across the floor. Despite her gloom, Elizabeth couldn't help being impressed; Celia was a vision out of the court of Louis XV. "There," her aunt said, coming to a graceful stop. "See how simple it is? Come, dear, try it again."

Taking a deep breath, Elizabeth walked to the closet and back. Her satin slippers didn't have excessively high heels, but she still listed dangerously. "I feel like a little girl dressed up in her mother's clothes," she complained wobbling back. "How did they ever manage all these skirts in those days?"

"For one thing they didn't bob about so. Float—like this—as if you were balancing a tray of eggs on your head."

"If I had eggs up there they'd be scrambled. My hair weighs a ton and I'm six feet tall instead of five foot six. Did you have to put a cushion on top?"

"We had to add to the height. It was quite the *done* thing in the eighteenth century. Stop frowning, darling, it's making your patches slip."

Elizabeth touched the small black circle of silk Celia had glued beside her mouth. A second patch had been placed slightly below her right eye. "I look like I've got the measles."

Celia groaned. "Darling, do stop fussing. Anyone would think I was making you walk the plank instead of bringing you to the most exciting ball of the season." She rearranged a loose curl on Elizabeth's forehead. "You look ravishing, dear. It's a shame you have to wear a mask, but that is part of the fun, isn't it?"

Celia examined herself one last time in the mirror, then pronounced them both ready. "Just remember, Elizabeth, glide evenly. And for heaven's sake, stop tugging at your skirts."

This advice was well and good for Celia, Elizabeth brooded as she tried to find a comfortable position during the short water taxi ride to the Venetian Palace, the fifteenth-century palazzo turned hotel where tonight's ball was being held. Celia's glide was naturally smooth—no scrambled eggs there—and her voluminous skirts were miraculously well behaved.

For her part, Elizabeth's black lace mask kept slipping down over her eyes making it difficult to see, and her head ached from the pins, powder and fillers her aunt had used. Worst of all, her underclothing continued to itch, and no matter how she sat or how hard she pushed at it, the darn hoop kept popping up. After listening to Celia's repeated instructions on how a proper lady managed such things, Elizabeth gave up and stood for the remainder of the trip.

The ballroom was already crowded by the time they arrived—the better to make an entrance, Celia explained—and music from a twenty-piece orchestra set a fitting backdrop for the fantasy-like setting. Huge crystal chandeliers lit the gilt-and-damask rococo interior. Gold glittered everywhere, from the gilded stuccos and elaborately paneled ceiling to the statuary and magnificent old paintings that decorated the walls. It was a real-life fairy tale, an unexpected peek into Venice's golden past.

All around Elizabeth revelers dressed as dukes and duchesses, harlequins, white-faced Pierrots, cupids, animals and any number of red-suited devils sporting long tails and pitchforks. For the first time since donning powder and hoop she did not feel self-conscious. In fact, she spotted so many other Marie Antoinettes that she silently blessed Celia for borrowing such a popular costume. Despite Celia's scolding, she intended to melt into the background and watch the extravaganza from the sidelines. In fact, if she took notes, the evening might be of some use after all. This was just the sort of affair Miss Amore could use in one of her books.

At the first opportunity, Elizabeth slipped away from her aunt. She had already chosen her spot, a far corner of the room away from the orchestra and behind the bust of an early doge, or Venetian ducal magistrate. From here she had a clear view of the dancers yet was out of the line of traffic. She had just pulled a small notebook out of her reticule when a round little waiter dressed as a frog popped his head behind the statue.

"Champagne, *signorina*?" he asked, offering her a glass of sparkling beverage.

Elizabeth shook her head. "No, thank you. I don't drink champagne."

"Take, take," the waiter persisted. "You like."

"No, I won't like. It tickles my nose and gives me a headache."

"No, *signorina*. Not for nose. To drink—see, like this." The little waiter made a great show of sipping from one of the glasses. Beaming at her, he again pressed the drink into her hand. "You take. Very nice. *Delizioso*."

"I don't want any. Really." It was no use, the little frog was not going to take no for an answer. He'd be the perfect match for Celia, Elizabeth thought ruefully. With a resigned sigh, she gave in and accepted the glass. "Thank you, *signore. Grazie*."

A broad smile lit his round face. "*Prego, signorina*. You enjoy, you see."

Elizabeth nodded and tipped her glass at him doubtfully, a gesture that occasioned a broad wink and a profusion of rapid Italian. When he had finally waddled off, she took a tentative sip of the champagne and, finding no place to deposit the drink, finished it off and put the empty glass on the floor next to the pedestal. Readjusting her mask for the dozenth time, she again took out her notebook and pen and settled down behind the statue to observe.

Two

———

Roberto Roselli was bored. Paradoxically, the fact that the party was one of the highlights of *Carnevale* merely added to his discontent. Tonight's ball was completely indistinguishable from the others he had attended since arriving in Venice—or the ones in London and France for that matter. Costumes varied, of course, as did accents and settings. But basically they were all the same. Boring!

Roberto lifted a whiskey from a passing waiter—anything to save him from one more drop of champagne—took a long sip, then surveyed the room from beneath the wide-brimmed straw hat he wore as part of his gondolier costume. Across the dance floor his practiced eye took in two striking young women dressed as courtesans. For a moment he toyed with the idea of asking one of them to dance, then decided against it. Tonight he had no interest in dancing or in the idle flirtation the young ladies would expect. Tonight he was not in the mood for any of this!

He turned away from the women in self-disgust. What was the matter with him? Roberto was twenty when, fifteen years ago, he'd lost his father. Since then he had worked single-mindedly to get where he was today. He had fought to rebuild his family's holdings and, more importantly, their reputation for possessing the finest stable of horses in Europe. In the end he had succeeded beyond his wildest dreams. Now, at the pinnacle of his success, he was bored.

Suddenly the room was too warm, too crowded; Roberto had a need to be away from the bright lights and the trendy guests. He finished his drink and started across the room. But before he could slip outside, his attention was caught by a glitter of gold coming from a corner near the door. Looking more closely he saw that a young woman was standing there, the folds of her gold-brocade gown peeping out from behind an ugly bust of Doge Grimani to catch the light from a chandelier. His first thought was that she was waiting for someone, her lover perhaps. Then, something about the way she held herself behind the statue caused him to change his mind. This was no romantic assignation. The woman was deliberately hiding!

"What have we here?" he murmured, his interest piqued. Maneuvering for a better look, Roberto was surprised to see the woman pull a pen from the depths of her elaborate hairdo and scribble something in a book. As she bent her head, the lacy mask she wore slipped over her eyes and she pushed at it absently with her hand. She seemed unaware that these actions disarranged her hair and sent a black beauty patch fluttering to the floor.

Boredom forgotten, Roberto amused himself by trying to identify the mystery woman. Since he had at least a passing acquaintance with most of the women at the ball, he decided she was not part of the usual crowd. He was certain he would have remembered such a superb figure. More practically, she didn't act like any of the women who normally frequented his circle. No woman he knew would dress up this magnificently merely to hide behind a statue and take notes!

Since Roberto had a weakness for puzzles—and what more delightful puzzle than the mystery of a beautiful woman?—he set his mind to solving this one. The first move, of course, was to ask the young lady to dance. And after that... Roberto's fertile imagination presented him with several intriguing possibilities, each more than capable of transforming a boring evening into one ripe with promise. Before he could put the first step of his plan into action, however, Celia Randolph bore down on him, her handsome face glowing from beneath several pounds of powdered curls and a profusion of jewels.

"Roberto! There you are. I was sure you'd be dancing."

"Another moment and I would have been." Despite the poor timing, Roberto was pleased to see Celia. Unlike most women her age—who seemed determined to railroad all eligible bachelors into marital bliss—Celia was refreshingly intelligent and blessed with an outrageous sense of humor. Better still, she knew enough to stay out of other people's business.

Until now.

"I'm glad I caught you," she said, taking his arm conspiratorially. "There's someone I want you to meet."

Roberto could not repress a groan. "Not you, too, Celia. You were the one woman I thought I could trust."

"After you've met her you'll thank me. She's beautiful."

"The good Lord help us, they're all beautiful."

"And boring," she said with a twinkle in her green eyes. "Come now, Roberto, admit it. You're bored to death."

He looked at her sharply, surprised she had stumbled so close to the truth. "Why do you say that?"

"Believe me, darling, you've got all the signs. Which is why I decided to introduce you to my niece."

Merciful Madonna, a niece! "Sorry, Celia, I've already chosen my next dance partner."

"Don't be ridiculous. The last thing you need is another fawning female with a big bustline and an empty head. My niece is blessed with brains and a healthy measure of common sense—perhaps too much of the latter," she added more to herself than to him. "You'll find her a welcome breath of fresh air."

Forgetting that the niece's good qualities were two of the very ones he most admired in Celia, Roberto conjured up an uncharitable vision of Celia Randolph's relative. "Actually, I'm rather tired, Celia. Perhaps some other time."

"Nonsense, what better time than the present?" She requisitioned a glass of champagne and placed it in his hand. "Don't go away. I'll only be a minute."

At first Roberto didn't know whether to be angry or amused by Celia's high-handed manipulations. Then the humor in the situation triumphed and he laughed. "But this time you will not win, dear Celia," he said beneath his breath, putting down the untouched drink. Tonight he was in no mood for intelligent, sensible nieces. Not even Celia Randolph's.

Still chuckling, he strode to the nearest exit, closed the door firmly behind him and walked out into the night.

Elizabeth was almost enjoying herself. After three champagne cocktails the evening was looking decidedly brighter. Not that she'd had any intentions of drinking so much, but the funny frog-waiter who kept poking his head behind the statue simply wouldn't take no for an answer.

"If I kissed you would you turn into Prince Charming?" she asked him as he pressed yet another glass into her hand.

"Preence?" he repeated with a heavy accent. *"Non capisco, signorina."*

"Prince, ah *primo.*" No, that wasn't right. *"Principe.* Do-you-turn-into-a-prince?" she repeated slowly.

The man looked even more confused. "No Preence in Italy," he told her earnestly. "Italy Republic—like America. Much freedom. Very nice."

"I'm sure it is," she said, taking a long sip of her drink before it spilled. "No preence, but lots of frogs." Overcome by laughter, she collapsed against the statue.

The waiter moved off, shaking his head at the strange *signorina* who came to the most celebrated ball of *Carnevale* merely to hide herself in a corner. On his blessed mother's grave he had done his best to draw her out. But it was clearly *impossible.* Americans! Who could understand them?

Elizabeth watched the little waiter waddle off, thinking that next to his comical way of speaking, the skinny little legs poking out of the padded middle of his frog suit were the funniest things she'd ever seen. If he only knew how silly he looked from behind, she thought, then stifled an unladylike burp. Oh, oh, I think you've had more than enough, Elizabeth my girl, she thought.

Balancing very carefully, she lowered herself and placed the nearly empty champagne glass next to a crooked little line of others that sat on the floor. She was just congratulating herself on a mission well done when Celia finally unearthed her prey.

"Elizabeth Bradshaw! What in the world are you doing hiding away back here? You're missing the entire party."

"I haven't missed a thing," her niece protested righteously. She waved her notebook as if to prove the integrity of this statement. "I'm preserving every glamorous moment for Miss Amore's thousands of devoted—" she repressed a burp "—oh, dear, excuse me, readers."

Celia raised an astonished eyebrow. "You've been drinking!"

"Only in the line of duty," Elizabeth explained with impeccable dignity. "I've been fostering American-Italian relations." She giggled. "A cute little frog keeps bringing me champagne hoping I'll turn him into a prince."

"My God, you're potted." Celia took her niece firmly by the shoulders and aimed her at the nearest powder room. "Get in there this minute and straighten up. Your hair's a mess, and somehow you've managed to lose one of your beauty marks. Hurry up. I want you to meet someone."

"Someone?" She strained to look back at Celia over her shoulder. "Is this a male someone or a female someone?"

"Roberto Roselli is very definitely a male." Refusing to be sidetracked, Celia continued to prod her niece in the right direction, but Elizabeth stubbornly dug in her heels.

"I don't want to meet any male someones. I'm into frogs tonight." She was giggling again and Celia was grateful they were hidden behind the marble doge. "I'll bet your someone won't turn into an Italian prince if I kiss him."

"He's already an Italian prince," Celia told her dryly. "Elizabeth, I've never seen you like this. What will Roberto think?"

A warning bell was ringing somewhere in the fog clouding Elizabeth's brain. "This Roberto of yours doesn't happen to play the ponies and collect stables full of beautiful women, does he?"

"Mr. Roselli is a very successful horse breeder," Celia replied, deciding the best way to get her niece into the ladies' room was to lead her there personally. "And most women find him exceedingly attractive. I'm sure you will, too." Reaching the powder room, Celia gave her niece a final push inside. "I'll be back to collect you in five minutes. For heaven's sake do something with your hair."

Since the room had started to move about disconcertingly, Elizabeth sank into the nearest chair. She closed her eyes until the room stopped spinning, then opened them to find a pale, unfamiliar face peering at her from the gilded mirror. She took in her wide, too bright eyes and groaned to herself, "My God, Elizabeth. How could you let this happen to you?"

A cursory inspection of her hair proved Celia right; it was a disaster. She poked at it more or less ineffectively, then, deciding she really didn't care what her hair looked like, gave up.

It wasn't working, she decided, staring at the doleful face in the mirror. She hadn't wanted to come to the party in the first place and look where it had gotten her: higher than the Alps and about to meet Europe's answer to Hugh Hefner. The champagne had begun to take its toll in more ways than a bad case of the giggles and spinning furniture. It felt as if a hundred tiny men with sledgehammers had decided to renovate her head. She was in no condition to meet Celia's society friends, least of all the infamous Lothario of the Italian Riviera.

"What you need, Elizabeth Bradshaw," she mumbled, making her way carefully to the door, "is fresh air. And bed. Yes, definitely bed. The hotel, a shower and bed!"

Weary of fighting with her mask, she tossed it into the trash on her way out of the powder room. With a surreptitious look around for Celia, she made her way across the room and out the door as quickly as fifteen pounds of dress and an eight-foot hoop would allow. It was only when the brisk February air hit her like a wall of ice that she realized she'd left without her wrap. Well, she'd just have to brave it, she decided, rubbing her arms briskly. There was no way she was going to risk seeing her aunt by going back to get it. Anyway, their hotel wasn't far. Soon she'd be in her own room tucked safely into bed, away from Celia, Carnival balls and especially Roberto Roselli!

That is if she could find a water taxi, she amended several very cold minutes later. Cursing the universal scarcity of taxis when you needed them, Elizabeth finally spied a gondola station and several men wearing the traditional striped shirt and straw hat uniform of the gondolier. Shivering, she hurried over to the nearest man.

"Excuse me. Ah, *mi scusi, signore,* but are you free?" She went on to name her hotel, then added, teeth chattering, "If you don't mind, could we please hurry?"

Roberto was so surprised to see his mystery woman that for a moment he didn't move. Then, realizing she must be freezing without a wrap, he thanked his good fortune which had prompted him to dress as a gondolier and led her to the nearest gondola. "You are cold, *signorina.* Quickly, into the boat."

As soon as she was settled in the seat, Roberto found a blanket and tucked it solicitously around her shoulders. Then, spying an angry gondolier hurrying toward them, he told her with an exaggerated accent, "You wait one moment, please," and nimbly intercepted the man before he could sound an alarm. "I'll have your boat back in one hour," he said, pressing several large bills into the gondolier's hand. "You will receive this much again when I return."

Leaving the startled gondolier on the dock, Roberto pushed the boat into the canal. The mystery woman's hotel was to the north. Without hesitation he set off to the south. As he experimented with the unfamiliar pole, Roberto was grateful he kept active at the stables. Pushing one was harder than it looked, and his admiration for the picturesque gondoliers rose as he struggled to establish a steady rhythm and at the same time keep out of the path of passing boats.

As he'd anticipated, she did not notice they'd taken off in the wrong direction. Roberto was standing behind her, but she was resting her head against the seat—eyes closed, blanket drawn up tightly to her chin. He had a clear view of her face and after negotiating a turn onto a less crowded canal, he took a moment to study her features in the moonlight. With a mutter of satisfaction, he congratulated himself on the accuracy of his original assessment. Despite the ridiculous bouffant hair and the layers of makeup, she appeared very young. And lovely. Yes, the woman of mystery was decidedly lovely.

"You are feeling warmer now?" he asked when she opened her eyes.

"Yes, thank you, much warmer," she said wriggling farther beneath the blanket. Now that she'd made a successful escape from the ball and was at least partially thawed, Elizabeth felt surprisingly cheery. There was something magical about the evening; maybe it was the stars, or the three-quarter moon, or the sounds of Carnival floating on the night air. Or perhaps it was the champagne, she thought, stifling a little giggle. Whatever the reason, she didn't see why she couldn't relax and enjoy it.

"Venice can be very cold in February," he told her. "You should not go out at night without a coat."

"I had a coat, but I left it behind when I ran away from the bully."

"Bully?"

"My aunt. The one who dragged me to the party." Her smooth brow creased into a frown. "Don't you just hate people who always have to have their own way?"

"Absolutely, *signorina*. It is a most annoying trait."

She sniffed. "It's more than annoying, it's un-American!"

They approached an intersection and the noises of Carnival increased as if an invisible hand had turned up the volume. Costumed revelers swelled across the bridge and in the distance Elizabeth could hear the sounds of a rock band. As they passed beneath the bridge span, a couple dressed as Aunt Jemima and a Turkish sheik waved to them. Elizabeth laughed and waved back.

"You have a lovely smile, *signorina*," he said. "As you see, *Carnevale* can be quite amusing."

"Out here it's wonderful," she said dreamily. "Venus Amore would love it."

"Venus Amore? There is actually a person with this name?"

"There certainly is. Miss Amore is a very famous author. *Un scrittrice romantico*," she said, sweeping her hand out dramatically. "And I, my dear Mr. Gondolier, am her trusted researcher."

"You are full of surprises, *signorina*. That must be fascinating work."

Elizabeth turned and placed a finger over her lips. "Shhh, no one's supposed to know I enjoy it. It would ruin my reputation in the Historical Society."

"The Historical Society?"

"Yes, indeed. I'll have you know you're transporting Colorado State's foremost expert in eighteenth-century European history. My article on the First Jacobite uprising was published in the *Wheat Ridge Globe*."

"I am impressed, *signorina*."

"Take Venice. I'll bet you didn't know that your Casanova spent several years in a religious seminary. Or that he introduced the lottery to Paris. Ah hah! I thought not. That was in Miss Amore's third book, *The Rape of Roxanne*."

"Your knowledge is astounding, *signorina*."

"Yes, I could tell you stories about some of the doges' debaucheries that would stand your hair on end." She looked around with hazy disorientation. "I don't remember coming this way from the hotel."

"The *rii* can be confusing," he said reassuringly. "I have taken an *atalho*, a shortcut, that is all."

"It seems like a longcut to me. Are you sure you're not abducting me, Mr. Gondolier?"

"I admit the idea is not an unpleasant one, *signorina*," he said, turning onto a relatively quiet side street. "However, you may relax. I am merely showing you Venice by moonlight. There is no extra charge, I assure you."

Elizabeth sighed and leaned back in her seat. Actually she didn't care how long the ride took—she could go on like this all night, drifting along the canal, with his soft, low voice relaxing her. "You've got a sexy voice, Mr. Gondolier," she said contentedly. "I can tell you're a real gentleman, an asset to international relations. Not like that horsey-set Don Juan my aunt tried to fix me up with at the party."

Roberto's face was hidden in the shadows. "Don Juan?"

"You know, gigolo—playboy." She turned around in her seat. "Would you like to hear my theory, Mr. Gondolier? I think Mr. Roselli spends too much time with his stallions. Some of it's rubbed off on him." Her head fell back and she collapsed with a fit of laughter.

Roberto kept his voice conversational. "Are you by any chance referring to Roberto Roselli, *signorina*?"

"That's the one. My aunt thinks he's utterly mah-vah-lous. Which just goes to show that even the great Celia Randolph can be taken in by a smooth line."

"Celia Randolph? She is your aunt?" Elizabeth was too busy watching some cats race across a bridge to hear the note of astonishment in his voice. "Now that truly is amazing."

"Oh, I don't know. Actually Celia's a pretty ordinary name, although *this* Celia is anything but ordinary." She giggled. "Mother calls her kooky, but then she goes through husbands the way some people change their hats and is in no position to throw stones. Do you know why there are so many cats in Venice?"

"Cats?"

"Yes, in case you haven't noticed they're all over the place. Maybe it's because you've got so many pigeons, huh?" She was giggling again. "Did you know he collects trophies?"

"He? You mean for the cats?" Her conversational jumps were making him dizzy.

"No, I mean Roberto Roselli. There was a picture of him in the paper the other day holding two of them, a blonde one and a—" she was overcome by another fit of laughter "—and a redhead. Do you suppose—do you suppose he keeps those photos on his mantle along with his horse ribbons?"

"You disapprove very strongly of this Mr. Roselli."

"In Marie Antoinette's day he would have been called a blackguard and some jealous husband would probably have shot him in a duel. He feeds on women, Mr. Gondolier."

"Those are harsh words for a man you have not even met."

"I don't have to meet him to know his type. Oh, look! There's the band." They had turned a bend in the canal and she could see a musical group playing in front of a café. "Let's stop, please," she cried impulsively. "I want to dance."

"As you wish, *signorina*," Roberto said, taken aback to find himself the unwitting villain of their conversation. Horsey Don Juan indeed, he thought in angry indignation. He had never "fed" off a woman in his life!

"You know something, Mr. Gondolier," she told him as he coolly helped her out of the boat. "You're too serious. This is *Carnevale*. You've got to loosen up."

Leaving Roberto standing openmouthed behind her, Elizabeth happily joined the throng. There were so many people crowding the sidewalk that she didn't feel the least bit cold. Tossing the blanket back into the boat, she accepted the hand of a masked Pantalone and started to dance. She had taken only a couple of steps, however, when she was firmly pulled away by the gondolier.

"Didn't your aunt tell you not to dance with strangers?" he asked, severely tempted to give the opinionated *signorina* a sound shaking. Then he found himself distracted by the soft rise of her breasts above the low-cut gown, and these thoughts gave way to more amorous designs. There was, perhaps, a more pleasant way to teach the young lady a lesson.

"But you're a stranger," she managed between turns.

"I'm a gentleman, remember? An asset to international relations." The hand on her back slid down a notch. "Besides, as you pointed out it's *Carnevale* and I have a sudden urge to loosen up."

With remarkable ease he swept them both into the beat of the music. Forced to hold her at some distance due to the cumbersome folds of her gown, Roberto nonetheless led her so skillfully that she almost forgot she was wearing the costume. "You dance beautifully," she told him dreamily. "I wish you could have been my partner at the ball."

"Ah, that would have been most improper, *signorina*."

"Yes, wouldn't it," she said, laughing. "Imagine what Roberto Roselli would have thought if I'd danced with you instead of him. Celia would have had a fit!"

She expected him to share her amusement. Instead, she found him staring at her with a peculiar expression on his face. And what a face! With a little shock Elizabeth realized how handsome the gondolier was. Without knowing it, she seemed to have stumbled upon a hero right out of a Venus Amore novel.

In the interest of research, she felt duty bound to examine her remarkable find more closely. Like all the author's heroes he was very tall, and beneath the close-fitting shirt and trousers she suspected that his muscular arrangement would more than meet with Miss Amore's approval. His hair was nearly black—another good point—and curled around a strong, pleasantly angular face. Dark brows, which were just bushy enough to be forceful, arched over smoky-gray eyes. An amused, no, *sexy* smile played at the corners of full, faintly mocking lips. He was reminiscent of Rogue Barlow, Miss Amore's latest paladin.

"Oh!" A push from the crowd abruptly ended Elizabeth's inspection and sent her careening into his arms. As he steadied her she felt an unexpected draft on the back of her legs and an embarrassed moment later realized that her hoop, and her skirts, must be flying high behind her. Revealing—oh my goodness!

Hastily, Elizabeth broke away from him and pushed the hoop back in place. "Crowded, isn't it?" she said, uncomfortably aware she was blushing.

"Yes, it is," he agreed, keeping hold of her hand. Gently he ran the tips of his fingers beneath the exquisite lace sleeves and up her arm. Needle-sharp prickles raised up all over her body and she gave an involuntary little jump. What was happening to her? Escape, Elizabeth, escape! a little voice screamed inside her head. "It's—it's late," she stammered. "I should be getting back to the hotel."

"As you wish, *signorina*." Promptly he released her and led the way back to the gondola. While he again arranged the blanket about her shoulders, she felt an irrational stab of disappointment. Did he have to be this honorable? The heroes in Miss Amore's books rarely acted with so much propriety. At least he could have put up a token argument.

The rest of the journey was made in silence. The sights and sounds of Carnival were gradually fading as he slipped the boat next to the stairs leading up to her hotel. Confused by the battle waging inside her, Elizabeth didn't know

whether to be frustrated or relieved that the ride was over.
He took her hand and led her off the boat.

"Thank you," she told him, feeling that the words were
inadequate but not having the vaguest idea what else to say.

"No, *signorina*, it is I who should thank you." To her
dismay—or was it to her delight? she wondered in confusion—he again kept hold of her hand. "Seeing *Carnevale* through your eyes has made it fresh and exciting."

"Yes, it's been fun." Her body was behaving badly again.
Her heart was pounding, her mind whirling. His voice
touched her like a physical caress, and his eyes were dark,
shimmering pools in the moonlight. Watch out, she warned
herself. Do not look into those eyes. They're dangerous!

To mask her confusion, Elizabeth managed to extricate
her hand and pull out her old-fashioned reticule. "How
much do I owe you?"

"No, no, *signorina*. Please, you owe nothing. It has been
my pleasure."

"But of course I owe you something. If you'll just tell me
how much—oh!" He had placed his hand on her waist and,
unmindful of the ungainly hoop, he was pulling her toward
him. He stopped when their bodies were lightly, almost im-
perceptibly, touching. From the sudden chill on her legs,
Elizabeth knew her skirts must once again be flying, but this
time she was incapable of moving away from him.

"You are beautiful, *signorina*," he told her softly.

"So are you," she said breathlessly.

She heard his chuckle as he bent his head to meet hers.
His hand moved behind her neck, tilting it to meet his lips,
and to her astonishment Elizabeth found herself standing on
tiptoes to meet his embrace. I want him to kiss me, she
thought in shocked realization. I want to know what it's like
to have a man like this take me in his arms.

His mouth descended and everything but the magical
touch of his lips faded from her mind. The kiss was hardly

more than a brush but she was astonished by its power to shake her. Like cool satin his lips pressed against hers and thousands of tingles spread deliciously through her body. Was this what it was like to have an *affare passione*? she wondered distractedly. After all the novels, after all the fiery love scenes, would she finally find out what it was really about?

"What are you doing to me?" she murmured when he gave her a moment to breathe.

"I thought that was obvious, *signorina*," he whispered against her mouth. "I am making love to you."

"Oh." She closed her eyes as his breath laced with hers, then she felt her heart jump when they touched. Soft, persuasive strokes parted her lips and his tongue slipped inside. As if he were playing a delicate instrument he traced sensuously over the line of her teeth, then across the sensitive curve of her inner cheek. His soft murmurs in Italian sent liquid fire through her veins, and she clung to his shoulders as if they were a lifeline.

But the feel of his hard muscles merely added fuel to her already smoldering senses. She was losing ground, slipping away under the skillful probing of his tongue. Expertly he drew her into the embrace, teasing her into full participation. Her tongue sought his and she felt the scoring heat of it until she lost the ability to think and could only feel.

She was doing that entirely too well. He filled her senses; never had she been so aware of a man. His hands burned through the heavy silk brocade to scorch her skin, and she felt an intense ache growing in the lower part of her body. What was happening to her? Sherman had never made her feel like this; sweet, serious, scholarly Sherman, whose kisses, like his personality, were always just a bit absent-minded. Through a fog of desire she knew there would never be anything tentative about the gondolier. Of all the heroes she might have stumbled upon, Elizabeth doubted she could have come upon one more dangerous. Do something before it's too late! her conscience shouted.

"Venice is built on one hundred and seventeen islets with one hundred and fifty canals and four hundred bridges," she rattled off, keeping her eyes tightly closed.

Roberto's head came up in surprise. "I beg your pardon?"

"From west to east it's 4,260 meters long, and from north to south, 2,790 meters wide." She opened a tentative eye to find him regarding her as if she'd taken leave of her senses. "It covers an area of 7,062 square kilometers."

"*Signorina*, what are you talking about?"

"The city—it was in my guidebook. Why me?"

He studied her face in the moonlight. She was waiting for his answer as if it were of earth-shattering importance. Despite the passion that burned through his body, he was touched by her efforts to remain in control. "You are *bellissima*, very desirable," he told her quietly. His tongue followed the outline of her lips with whisper-light softness. "Is that not reason enough?"

Elizabeth could think of at least a dozen reasons why it wasn't, but at the moment it was impossible to articulate a single one. She was so distracted by the way his hands were sculpting the shape of her body through the bodice of silken gown that she couldn't come up with any more statistics. When his fingers skimmed the sensitive underside of her breasts she caught her breath.

"Have you studied the topographical configuration of the city, Mr. Gondolier?" Her voice was a hoarse whisper. "I hear—I hear it's quite remarkable."

"I find your topography even more remarkable," he murmured against her ear. Through the cool fabric of her gown, his thumbs drew slow, wonderful circles around the tips of her nipples until she was certain the ache in her stomach would explode. He knew all the right answers and she was sinking for the third time.

"No," she moaned, and tried to push him away, aware through her confusion that what she was really struggling against was her irrational desire to melt into him until she could feel every inch of his wonderful body. He was dizzyingly close, a heartbeat away. It was impossible to deal logically with her feelings when his tongue was searching out the most secret recesses of her mouth, when his fingers were lightly massaging the curve of her neck. She shivered with pleasure.

"You are cold, *signorina*," he murmured, wondering at the exquisite softness of her skin. "I know a very pleasant way to keep warm. Would you like me to show you?"

"Yes—I mean, no. Oh, I don't know what I mean." His velvet-smooth voice, the seductive words, shook her to the core. The ache was spreading to her thighs and the need to do something about it was growing desperate. "Your hands—they're—I can't concentrate."

"You mean when I do this—" he lowered his head and let his lips follow the tingling path of his finger "—or this—" his tongue flickered over the smooth swell of her breasts "—or this?"

She gasped when his lips nudged the lacy edge of her bodice lower, driving the pounding need deep into her body. There wasn't a single part of her that didn't ache for him. This was crazy—a fantasy. Scenes like this didn't happen in real life. At least, not in the life of Elizabeth Marie Bradshaw, research historian from Wheat Ridge, Colorado. It really is madness, she thought in mounting dismay. I've got a severe case of Carnival madness!

"Please, don't." Every one of her senses remained acutely tuned to him as she forced her hands against his chest. "I don't even know you."

"But you will, *mia cara*. I promise you will know me very well." His voice purred through her senses. It took every ounce of will to maintain what little distance she had achieved.

"No, I won't. This is a dream. I'll never see you again." And I'll never forget you. I'll never forget you, or Venice, or this evening, for as long as I live.

"Why do you deny your emotions?" he asked, finding the sensitive pulse in her throat. "Your body does not lie. What is happening between us is not a dream." Beneath his fingers the traitorous beat took an erratic leap and she wondered how he could have such a devastating effect on her. This man was infinitely more dangerous than she'd thought.

"Emotions that have gotten out of hand should be—oh, dear, could you—please stop? It's hard to think clearly."

"As you wish, *signorina*." He moved his hand to her shoulder where it continued to shatter her concentration. "You are trembling, *mia gioia*. Why are you afraid?"

"I'm not afraid. I'm just being—" she swallowed hard as his fingers strayed dangerously close to her breasts "—sensible. Look," she said, trying to push away from him. "I can't think with your hands so close to—when your fingers touch my—I just don't do this sort of thing."

Roberto was surprised by the panic he heard in her voice, and he realized with a little jolt that what had started out as an amusing form of revenge had grown into something more dangerous, something he had not expected nor could totally comprehend. Looking at her closely he noted the quick rise and fall of her breasts, the confused eyes, the trembling lower lip. The lovely *signorina* was out of her depths. With sudden, disturbing clarity, he remembered her earlier description of him as a predatory Don Juan, and the image was unsettling enough to take some of the edge off his passion. Without a word he released her, then watched perplexed as she straightened her skirts in a flustered attempt at dignity.

"One cannot always plot a smooth course for one's emotions, *signorina*. Affairs of the heart frequently choose their own path. Surely you know that from your work."

She looked at him blankly for a moment. "You mean my work with Miss Amore? But I don't research *those* parts of the novels, I mean I wouldn't—I couldn't." She came to an embarrassed stop and Roberto was amazed to see that she was blushing. She cleared her throat. "Besides, that's fiction. This is real life."

"And romantic passion has no place in real life?"

"Only if you like being on a runaway train. Who needs that kind of chaos in their life?"

"A runaway train," he repeated thoughtfully. "I must admit I have never thought of it in quite those terms."

"Yes, well you should—think of it, I mean." She shivered. Now that his embrace no longer protected her, the night seemed very cold. Elizabeth hugged herself, hating the part of her that wished she could melt again into his warmth.

He longed to touch her, to enfold her in his arms and shelter her from the cold. But because his body still ached for her, he merely tilted her chin with the crook of his finger and studied her face in the moonlight. He saw the reflection of his own passion in her expressive, sapphire-blue eyes. He also read confusion and fear, and a surprising depth of vulnerability. Worldly and naive, a provocative combination. Although her identity was no longer a secret to him the mystery woman remained very much a mystery.

"Rest assured I will give this evening a great deal of thought, *signorina*," he promised her gravely. Her answering gaze was cautious; she looked like a small, frightened animal prepared to bolt. "You have much to learn, and I would very much like to be your teacher." He leaned down and placed a chaste kiss on her forehead.

"*Arrivederci, mia amore.* Until we meet again."

She started to object that the probabilities of that happening were extremely remote, but he was already gone. Elizabeth watched the gondola until it was swallowed up by the shadows. With a vague feeling of emptiness, she turned and entered the hotel.

Three

The little men with sledgehammers had obviously decided against merely renovating her head in favor of total demolition. Elizabeth opened heavy eyes the next morning to discover that what didn't throb ached, and what didn't ache felt decidedly queasy. So much for her entry into Venetian society.

After two aspirin and a prolonged soak in the tub, her thoughts had strayed from masked balls and too much champagne to the handsome gondolier. There they remained stubbornly entrenched until Celia announced the arrival of the breakfast trolley in their common sitting room. By the time Elizabeth had finished dressing her mood had fluctuated from incredulity to acute embarrassment to an elusive sense of gloom.

Since memories of the night before were disturbing enough to make her want to take up permanent residence beneath her bedcovers, the first two emotions were understandable. The third was more complex, involving as it did a good deal of personal honesty. The truth of the matter, of course, was that her reaction to the gondolier had been totally out of character, which was grounds enough for alarm without this ridiculous sense of loss over never seeing him again. The inescapable conclusion to be drawn from this insanity was that there were murky depths to Elizabeth Bradshaw heretofore untapped.

She was in no mood, however, to hear her aunt's personal verification of this discovery.

"Really, darling, your behavior last night was most peculiar." Celia was seated majestically at the table pouring coffee from a silver urn. This morning she was wearing a gold lamé negligee trimmed with purple ostrich feathers, high-heeled slippers to match and a dazzling display of jewelry. Waving a particularly large amethyst ring beneath Elizabeth's nose, she finished serving, then sat back and regarded her niece reproachfully. "Why did you disappear from the ladies' lounge?"

"I had a headache."

"I'm not surprised after all that champagne." She put down the coffeepot and eyed her niece pointedly. "Don't tell me you walked all the way back to the hotel without a coat."

Elizabeth made a show of buttering a roll although she hadn't the slightest interest in eating. "I took a gondola."

"And the ride took two hours? Don't look surprised, I talked to the night man when I came in. I was worried when you left the ball alone. It wasn't like you." She waited expectantly, but when further elaboration was not forthcoming, gave a long sigh. "Really, darling, you're making this very difficult. Carnival is a time of excitement, of romance. You're not going to meet any interesting men running off like that. Elizabeth, are you all right?"

"I'm—fine," Elizabeth gasped between coughs as the coffee sputtered its way down her windpipe.

Celia leaned across the table. "You look a bit peaked. Are you ill?"

"No, really, I'm fine." Elizabeth managed a smile. "I think I'll walk to some museums this morning. The fresh air will do me good."

"Museums!" Celia's green eyes rolled heavenward as if beseeching intervention from a higher power. "Elizabeth, this is a vacation, an opportunity to live out your fantasies. You can't waste it poking about in drafty old rooms."

"I would hardly call Napoleon's Gallerie dell'Accademia a collection of drafty old rooms. And I keep telling you I don't have any fantasies."

"That's nonsense and you know it. Every healthy young woman has dreams. Why do you fight it so?"

"I'm not fighting anything, Celia. I just want to make the most of my time in Venice."

"Well at least we're in agreement on that point. Which is why I've prevailed upon Roberto to join us for lunch."

Elizabeth looked at her aunt in horror. "Roberto? Not Roberto Roselli!" The gondolier had been bad enough. The last thing she needed now was a spoiled, egotistical playboy. "That's out of the question."

Even Celia's good nature had its limits. "And would you care to tell me why?" she asked, a dangerous edge to her voice.

"I've made other plans for lunch."

"Then break them." She paused, then went on in honeyed tones, "May I remind you, dear, that you are in Venice, the city of romance. I know from your work with this Amore person that you're familiar with this word, although you seem to be going to inordinate lengths to convince me otherwise. Mr. Roselli is my friend; you are my niece. I would appreciate it if you would humor me, just this once, and grace us with your presence for lunch.''

"Just this once!" Elizabeth came very near to choking again. Then she saw the determined gleam in Celia's emerald-green eyes and knew only a fool would pick up the gauntlet. "What time?" she asked, knowing from long experience when to admit defeat.

"One o'clock, in the hotel dining room. I'm shopping with friends this morning at Capellini's, but I'll be back in plenty of time." Her good humor restored, Celia delicately dabbed at her lips with a linen napkin, then rose gracefully from the table. "Be a dear, Elizabeth, and wear the blue knit dress. It's not quite so dreary as the rest of your clothes, and it matches your eyes. We do want to emphasize your best feature, don't we?" With a regal toss of her head, Celia glided through a flurry of ostrich feathers to her bedroom door.

"*Ciao*, darling," she said, blowing Elizabeth a kiss. "See you at one."

She didn't in the least care if the dress matched her eyes. Elizabeth examined the sapphire-blue knit dolefully in the elevator mirror and wondered what had possessed her to buy it in the first place. Blue was one of her best colors, but the dress had a tendency to cling in embarrassing places and was too tight across the chest. Not that Mr. Roselli was apt to notice what she was wearing anyway. With the flotilla of women he had chasing him back and forth across the Mediterranean she could probably show up in a flour sack and he wouldn't know the difference. At this point Elizabeth only wanted to get lunch over with as quickly and painlessly as possible and hope that her aunt would forget matchmaking for the remainder of the trip!

As she walked through the hotel lobby Elizabeth saw no sign of Celia, which wasn't all that surprising since her aunt notoriously lost track of time when she was shopping. Well that suits me just fine, Elizabeth thought, wishing she could have remained lost for another hour or two in the Academy Gallery. The works of Bellini and Carpaccio were preferable any day to the company of the notorious Mr. Roselli.

As usual the hotel dining room was crowded, and a number of people were grouped outside the restaurant waiting to be seated. Taking up a position across from the entrance, Elizabeth passed the time by studying the patrons, a good many of whom were dressed in colorful carnival costumes.

It was several moments before she noticed the tall, dark-haired man standing to the side of the doorway. Delayed shock sent her eyes flying back for a second look. Beneath the stylish, very expensive suit, was the superb body she had last seen wearing a red-and-white striped shirt and wide-brimmed straw hat. His face was turned at an angle, but there was no mistaking those gray eyes, that strong profile, the sexy mouth. It was him, her gondolier, the man who had the power to make her blood sizzle with one devastating look. My God, what was he doing here? And dressed like that!

At that moment he turned and saw her, and a half smile curved on his face. For several seconds Elizabeth was too shocked to move, then was jolted out of her trance when he showed every intention of coming over to speak to her. Flying across the hall, she intercepted him before he had taken half-a-dozen paces.

"What are you doing here?" she whispered. "My aunt will arrive any minute. She can't see you!"

Roberto had been prepared to face a certain amount of resentment concerning his masquerade the night before, but he was hardly prepared to be treated like a specter from a late-night horror film. The lovely *signorina* was looking at him wildly, and her eyes kept darting back and forth to the lobby as if she were afraid the devil himself might walk in. "You can't stay here," she went on in a loud whisper.

Somewhere inside Roberto a spark of mischief flamed to life. Looking pained he said, "Can it be that you are ashamed of a humble gondolier, *signorina*?"

"Of course not. I mean there's nothing to be ashamed of. It's just that my Aunt Celia wouldn't understand." Elizabeth was tugging at his sleeve, trying to move him away from the dining room door. "Look, can we talk about this some other time?"

"Does that mean you will have dinner with me tonight, my little pigeon?"

"It means I want you out of here!" She darted a frantic look at the door. "Please, she'll be here any minute. I can't imagine why you came in the first place."

By now thoroughly enjoying himself, Roberto assumed his best comic opera voice. *"Mia d'oro,"* he proclaimed loudly, "I had to see you. I cannot eat, I cannot sleep. My heart, it pines for you. Tell me you have not forgotten our night of *grand passione*."

If there had been a foxhole available, Elizabeth would have gratefully sank into it. Curious heads were turning and the *capocameriere*, the headwaiter, was frowning in their direction. If Celia turned up right now the consequences would be too awful to think about.

"Tell me you have not foresaken me, my little dove. What we shared last night is etched forever upon my soul. I can still taste the nectar of your lips, feel the tender warmth of your—"

"Will you please shut up!" she growled through clenched teeth. An amused crowd had gathered around them, vocal in their enjoyment of the lover's tiff. Some of the men were encouraging Roberto in Italian. She didn't understand the language, but their blatantly obvious gestures required no translation. Driven beyond the boundaries of desperation, she grabbed his arm and before he could utter one more outlandish syllable, pushed, pulled and coerced him out of the hotel. Even there it wasn't safe; Celia might happen along at any second. She continued to prod him on until they blended into the crowd that filled St. Mark's Square.

"Ah, you want to run away with me, my little dove," he crooned when she paused to catch her breath. Taking advantage of her momentary weakness, he pulled her into his arms. "You are so impetuous, my love. So *romantica*."

"No, I'm not the least bit romantic." She tried unsuccessfully to squirm out of the embrace. "That's just the point. If Celia should see us I'd never be able to live it down."

"But you have written many books on love, *mia bella*. Why do you toy with me? My heart, it is devastated."

"Look, you've got to stop going on like this. I don't write books on love, I research them."

"But last night—"

"Last night was a mistake. It was, it was—" Despite the idiotic melodrama he was enacting, she found herself irresistibly drawn to him and his remarkable gray eyes. Right now they smiled at her with an expression she couldn't quite understand, a look she found so disturbing she lost her train of thought.

"Extraordinary? Magical? Unforgettable?" His voice was like a caress as his mouth ventured closer. "Of course, my sweet, you are right. It was all of these."

"Yes, well." She cleared her throat as his breath brushed her cheek and was dismayed to feel her body temperature soar. Even in broad daylight he was dangerous. What was worse, this morning she couldn't blame her runaway emotions on too much champagne. "What happened last night was—not the sort of thing I usually do."

"I would be very happy to change that, my love," he told her in a devastating purr. He rubbed the back of his forefinger down her cheek and the shock of his touch compressed her chest until she could hardly breathe. "You are even lovelier by daylight. The sun fires your hair with gold. And your lips—" He kissed his fingers dramatically. *"Magnifico!"*

"No. Not *magnifico*. And please stop calling me your love." Too distracted to notice the flock of pigeons that were conducting an intensive exploration of their shoes, she pulled back to find her feet hampered by half-a-dozen plump birds. Over a cacophony of indignant squawks and wildly fluttering wings, his firm arms broke her fall.

"Do not be shy, my little rosebud. Very soon you will be my love, my true, my one and only *amore*."

Elizabeth flailed about until she had pulled out of his arms. "Will you stop saying that? And you've got to forget about last night; it should have never happened. I can assure you that—" the sweep of her gaze locked onto a pair of brilliant orange plumes sailing high above an ivory-brocaded Poiret turban. No need for Elizabeth to look twice; there couldn't be two hats like it in all of Venice. Aunt Celia!

"Quick," she cried. "Follow me."

Having already spied the telltale plumage, Roberto offered no resistance as she pushed him through the first open doorway. Only after they were inside did either of them realize they had entered the Campanile, or bell tower.

"Maybe she didn't see us," Elizabeth said, closing her eyes and leaning against the wall for support. "Now will you please leave while there's time?" Feeling no movement beside her she opened her eyes to find him gone. No, not gone. There he was standing at the counter buying tickets for the tower elevator!

"What are you doing?" she cried, as he accepted the small slips of paper and pocketed the change. "I'm not going up there."

"You are trying to avoid someone, *signorina*," he said, leading her to the elevator. "From above it is possible to see the entire city."

Before she could raise the obvious objection that it was hardly necessary to view an entire city to dodge one determined aunt, they were in the lift and rising to the bell tower's three-hundred-and-twenty-foot height. When the elevator opened, he led her out to a panoramic sight. Below, the city and the lagoon stretched out as far as the eye could see.

"No wonder Montaigne called Venice 'that famous beauty,'" she said, forgetting everything else in sheer awe of the view. "It's breathtaking."

"From a distance it is beautiful, yes." Roberto felt a vague regret that he could no longer find Venice enchanting. Perhaps he had seen it too often, or looked at it too closely. For him it had become a hodgepodge of eras, of styles, living together in less than total harmony.

"Look! There's the Clock Tower, and the Ducal Palace. And across the canal Palladio's basilica. It's magnificent, like a beautiful painting."

Roberto followed the path of her arm, but could not match her enthusiasm. Despite the carnival revelry going on below the piazza seemed flat and unreal. "Not everyone would agree with you, *signorina*. Venice has been termed a gold idol with clay feet. Perhaps it strives too hard to be picturesque."

"But that's just the miracle, don't you see? Think of its history—formed by merchants whose sole interest was profit. How did people like that create this masterpiece? By rights Venice should be ugly. Yet look, it's a fairy-tale city, a fantasy."

Her eyes were shining, and Roberto felt a moment's envy that she could feel such unbridled passion for a city. Where had his own exuberance gone? he wondered. When had the skepticism, the boredom, set in?

"Here, it's the twentieth century that's out of place," she went on, too excited to notice his preoccupied musing. "Venice is like a priceless gem displayed in a unique antique setting. It's only when the outside world invades with its space-age gadgetry that it appears incongruous."

"You are opposed to progress, *signorina*?"

"I see no reason to alter something which is, in its own way, already perfect. Would the Venus De Milo be any more exquisite if a sculptor gave it new arms?"

The obvious truth to this statement left no room for comment, still it disturbed him. "I must admit that is an unusual perspective."

She was following the winding course of the Grand Canal with her finger. "Being a native, you're probably too close to the city to remain objective. And of course I'm not saying it's without flaws. Venice invented the income tax and gambling casinos, as well as the ghetto." She tilted her head and squinted. "I think it looks more like an eel than an S, don't you?"

"I beg your pardon?"

"The Grand Canal. All the guidebooks say it curves like an inverted letter S, but I think it squiggles like a long, slithery eel."

She turned from the canal to find him watching her closely. The sun fell across his face to accentuate the strong bone structure, the lean cheeks, the small crevice that divided his chin, the classic Roman nose. Perhaps it was seeing him clearly by daylight, but she had the odd feeling they'd met before. But try as she might, Elizabeth couldn't put a name or a place to the memory. There was an underlying impression of inconsistency, though; something wasn't quite right. "It just occurred to me that I don't even know your name."

"My mother called me Carlo," he told her, not adding that his mother had been the only person to address him by his middle name. He had seen the flicker of recognition cross her face and thought it just as well to skirt the truth a bit. "And your name, *signorina*?"

"Elizabeth. Elizabeth Bradshaw." She gave him a long, direct look. Dressed in a suit and tie there was little to remind her of last night's gondolier. She was also bemused by the fact that in the past few minutes he seemed to have lost most of his pronounced Italian accent. As a matter of fact, studying him now he didn't seem the least bit frivolous, not at all the sort of man to make a public scene. The situation suddenly struck her as very strange. "Why did you create that spectacle at the hotel?" she asked, eyeing him narrowly.

She saw the secret amusement on his face and the truth dawned with a flash of anger. "You did it on purpose, didn't you? Just to embarrass me."

That brought on a broad smile. "No, really. I *would* like to have dinner with you tonight."

"I mean all the rest of it—the 'I can't eat, I can't sleep, my heart it pines for you' nonsense." She felt her cheeks flame, and the knowledge that her face was such a dead giveaway for her feelings fueled her temper. "You deliberately made fun of me."

"I am a man, and you are a very desirable woman," he pointed out calmly. "At the time it seemed the best way to get you alone."

"Get me alone! You made a fool of me, made me miss a luncheon date with my aunt and her guest, just to get me alone? Why you overweening, self-centered—sadist! How dare you."

"You are aware, of course, that at present it is you who are creating the spectacle?" he pointed out with maddening serenity.

Looking around, Elizabeth was appalled to discover they had once again become the center of attention. Quickly she lowered her voice, but if looks really could kill he wouldn't have had a chance. "You're despicable."

"And you are very lovely when you're angry."

Her mouth opened to voice a not-so-very polite retort. "Oh, oh, I wouldn't say that if I were you." His eyes rolled to indicate their audience. "Of course, if we were to pretend to be lovers they would soon lose interest."

"I'll pretend no such thing. You're crazy!"

"Crazy with love for you, *mia gioia*," he boomed, resuming his stage voice. "Ah, my precious one, how can you be so cruel, so heartless?"

"All right, all right. You win. But for heaven's sake behave yourself."

"It would be easier to behave myself if you'd put your arms around me. And if you were to kiss me, I would be absolutely *angelico*."

"You didn't say anything about a kiss."

The hidden laughter in his voice was infuriating. "But what else would lovers do, my darling? Unless of course you would prefer to continue our performance for these good people."

Angrily, she moved closer. "You know I wouldn't." She screwed her eyes tightly closed. "All right, but be quick about it."

"Elizabeth—that is a lovely name—if you would try not to look as if I were about to do something sordid to your honor I think we would be more convincing."

She opened one eye and looked at him blankly.

"Your arms. Put them around me," he instructed.

With a withering look, she raised her arms and placed them around his neck. Then, despite her anger, she was dismayed to find herself sidetracked by his subtle, spicy scent and the feel of the hard muscles she remembered so clearly from the night before. Maybe this wasn't such a good idea, she thought, beginning to panic. Her pulse was pounding crazily again, and that awful, wonderful ache had returned to the pit of her stomach. What was it about this man that turned her nerves to jelly?

"You hold me as if I might bite." His voice was a delicate assault that flowed through her spine like tiny slivers of ice. He used his index finger to raise her chin, and the look in his eyes abruptly melted the ice and sent it coursing at the boiling point throughout her body. "I have not bitten anyone since Maria Carmagnola's third birthday party. I promise, you are perfectly safe."

Not so, not so, her inner voice contradicted. Elizabeth, my girl, you are about as safe as a canary at a cat convention. "Do you have to hold me so close?"

"Would you rather be a spectacle?"

"This is blackmail, you know."

His answer was a throaty chuckle that was lost against her mouth. When his lips came to her she felt the warming of his breath, then a shock as her surprised body pulsed to life. This afternoon there was nothing the slightest bit tentative about the kiss. There was instant heat, a spontaneous mating of their tongues, as if they knew there might not be enough time to savor and experience all that was available to them.

Desire washed over her in deep, hot waves, and she was nearly overcome by a need to know him, to feel his warmth against her. Last night she had rationalized these feelings by blaming them on too much champagne. Today there were no ready excuses, only the naked truth. This man was showing her more passion than she had ever dreamed existed. Sherman's kisses seemed like mere child's play by comparison. Here was excitement beyond her wildest imagination.

Here, too, she told herself with a frightening flash of clarity, was an unaccountable degree of danger, a menace she wasn't at all sure she was prepared to handle.

Four

——

It's not working," Elizabeth said when he gave her room to breathe.

"Of course it is." His lips brushed her mouth. "It is working very well."

"No, I mean them." She nodded toward their audience who, if anything, seemed more interested in the reconciliation than they had been in the fight. "They're still watching us."

"Let them." He was busy nuzzling her ear.

Drawing together the cloak of her tattered dignity, she pushed away from him, then crossed unsteady arms across her chest in an unconscious gesture of defense. "I can't. It makes me uncomfortable. *You* make me uncomfortable."

His firm hands kept hold of her shoulders, forcing her to look at him. "What you're really trying to say is that *men* make you uncomfortable, isn't it, Elizabeth?"

She started to shake her head in denial, then changed it to a doleful nod.

"Why?"

Elizabeth hesitated, not sure how to answer him. Her eyes drifted over the city as if the explanation were hiding somewhere below, outside herself. It was a cool day, sunny and unusually clear for February. In the piazza a troupe of mimes was performing in wooden masks. The crowd cheered and she had a sudden feeling of separation, as if she were watching a performance of people watching a performance. A spectator, wasn't that what Celia called her? Always watching life from the sidelines, careful to keep her distance lest she become involved and get hurt. She wished she knew the answer to his question.

"That's difficult. I've never been very good around men. I guess I don't completely trust them. I always wonder what they want from me. Dad left home when I was six, but I've had any number of stepfathers." She gave a nervous little laugh. "You'd think I'd be used to men, wouldn't you? Celia says I don't give them a chance."

"And do you?"

She sighed. "I don't know. I suspect it's more complicated than that. I've spent a lot of time thinking about it, planning my life. I don't want someone to come along and jeopardize everything I've worked for."

"So you avoid falling in love."

"I'm not sure I know what love is. I've read about it in books, but in real life it's not the same. It colors reality and makes people believe everything is rosy when it isn't. As a little girl I remember thinking: when I grow up I won't let some man make a lot of promises and then suddenly walk out of my life. I'll be careful who I give my heart to." She stopped, embarrassed, suddenly realizing that she'd never in her life shared these thoughts with someone, not even with Sherman. "I don't know why I'm telling you all this. You can't possibly be interested."

"Oh, but I am. I'm very interested to know if you have found such a man."

Unbidden, a picture of Sherman came into her mind. She was ashamed when it was accompanied by a fleeting flicker of doubt. When she answered she realized her voice sounded unnaturally bright. "Yes, I have. His name is Sherman and he's a research librarian back in Wheat Ridge." Even to her it sounded dull.

"You have chosen this Sherman with your head, not your heart."

"I've tried to keep my marriage in perspective. Sometimes I think people give more thought to buying a car than they do to choosing a lifetime partner."

"And you never worry about missing the passion, the excitement of an emotional relationship?"

Celia had said nearly the same thing in the Lacock tearoom. Clearly the romantics in the world were ganging up on her. "I care a great deal about Sherman. We're very close. But I think other more realistic considerations are equally important for a lasting relationship. Passion is fleeting," she added, thinking of her parents. "And emotions have been known to be wrong."

"Yet you work for a famous romance writer. That does not strike you as incongruous?"

"My personal views have nothing to do with my professional life. Miss Amore likes my research; I like her paychecks. It's an eminently practical relationship."

"I see." A subtle light came into his eyes that warned her he might be seeing too much. "Last night on the canal you admitted you enjoyed this work."

"It allows me to travel," she said, not looking at him. "And gives me time for my own research. Right now I'm doing a paper on ancient megalithic monuments," she added, hoping to turn the conversation on to more scholastic channels.

"Passion among the rocks?"

She flushed. "No, it's not for Miss Amore. It's my own work."

"Oh. Do you know something? I think I like my idea better." His arm had remained on her shoulder. Sensing her tension he found the sensitive area just below her hairline and began to massage it gently. With long, slow strokes, his fingers fanned out over her upper back and shoulders. He could not see her face but he felt her body stiffen. Very softly he asked, "Elizabeth, am I making you uncomfortable again?"

His talented fingers were working miracles on her knotted muscles, but the warm, wonderful sensations that were spreading down from her shoulders were igniting more ominous fires in the lower regions of her body. In his hands even an innocent back rub took on the powers of an aphrodisiac. "No," she lied, taking a deep gulp of air. "It feels—good."

His warm breath fanned her neck and she gasped. "Relax, Elizabeth. There's nothing to be afraid of."

But there is, she thought. No one had ever made her feel like this before with so little effort. What had happened to the level-headed, rational woman who had arrived in Venice yesterday afternoon? Was it only yesterday! Since then her life had been turned upside down. A stranger had taken over her body and he said not to be afraid.

"Let me show you how to let go." The voice caressed her neck, her cheek, her senses. "You are missing so much by closing yourself off." He paused and her heart stopped beating. "I want to make love to you, *mia cara*."

Elizabeth heard the words in a kind of numb denial. I don't even know this man and he wants to make love to me. What's worse, I'm actually considering it!

A cool breeze off the canal touched her face. Looking down she saw a tourist in the piazza posing for a picture, his outstretched arms covered with pigeons. Watching him she thought, even while we stand up here calmly discussing what can be done to correct Elizabeth Bradshaw's inadequate sex life, the rest of the world rolls merrily on its way. It was unreal.

It took every ounce of her willpower to pull herself back to reality and say in an almost normal voice, "Do you think it's going to rain?" She pointed to the only cloud in the sky, an innocuous puff of white vapor so minute and so distant it couldn't have been counted on to water a flea.

With an almost inaudible sigh, his fingers stopped their assault. Keeping his hands on her shoulders, he turned her around until she was facing him. "Don't worry," he said, his gray eyes softening as if he understood her inner turmoil. "If it rains I will personally see to it that you remain warm and dry."

Looking into his face she again felt the jolting power of his appeal. His dark eyes enveloped her like a fiery caress, and for a brief, crazy moment she was tempted to succumb to the physical needs which, now that they'd been awakened, demanded gratification. Still weak from his massage she muttered unsteadily, "Yes, well I'd better be getting back to the hotel. Just in case. Besides," she added, realizing she must sound inane, "you don't have an umbrella."

"For what I had in mind an umbrella would not be necessary." An amused smile hovered on his lips as if he easily saw through her flimsy defenses. "If you would care to come to my room I would be happy to show you what I mean. So that you will feel more secure."

Secure! Elizabeth nearly laughed out loud. There was no way she would feel secure within a fifty-mile radius of this man. "Oh, look, here's the elevator now," she said, turning gratefully toward the creaking conveyance.

He took her arm, and she heard his faintly mocking voice as they got onto the lift, "We've lost our audience."

Elizabeth was surprised to discover she'd forgotten all about the onlookers. "We must have been too boring for them."

"We could liven things up again." He leaned down and started to touch her mouth with his lips when a sudden tide of passengers pushed into the lift throwing them together. They laughed, and Elizabeth felt a decreasing of the tension that had been building inside her.

"Too late. We've already been forgotten." She'd been pressed tightly against his chest and her cheek still rested against his shoulder. His proximity and the clean fragrance of his aftershave were making her lightheaded. Uneasily, she pulled away from him just as the elevator came to a bumpy stop. Across the square the clock tower was striking the hour as they stepped out onto the piazza. Elizabeth looked up at the two Moorish figures who marked the time on the fanciful clock in surprise. "We were up there over an hour. I can't believe the time passed so quickly."

"Yes, much too quickly."

Something in his voice sent her reflexes into instant alert, and the wary look that came into her eyes made him chuckle softly. Gently he took her hand, his gaze turning the muscles in her legs to jelly. "This afternoon, time was against us. Later perhaps, it will treat us more kindly." His mouth formed a sexy half smile that would have elevated any woman's blood pressure. "I want to know you better, Elizabeth Bradshaw. Much, much better."

He raised her fingers to his lips, and for a long moment she met his spellbinding gaze. Then, slowly, reluctantly he dropped her hand and walked off into the crowd.

"*Arrivederci*, Carlo," she whispered. He didn't look back, and she told herself she wouldn't, either. But as she made her way to the hotel the empty feeling was back stronger than ever. Elizabeth wondered how long it would be before it left.

"If you so much as move out of my sight I will disown your entire branch of the family!"

Celia flashed a dazzling smile to a British earl and his wife who passed them in the hall, then went on with her tirade as if there'd been no interruption. "Moreover, you will be charming to my friends. *All* my friends, Elizabeth. There will be no note taking, no long, dreary dissertations as to who took off whose head during the French revolution and no remarks, I mean absolutely none, about old rocks. Do I make myself clear?"

"Celia, it was only a lunch date, not the end of the world."

"Perhaps not, but it was embarrassing to be stood up, especially when it was for the second time in fifteen hours. And when Roberto didn't make an appearance either—" A long shudder. "Surely, Elizabeth, you can imagine my chagrin."

She could. Her aunt might be tolerance itself when it came to other people's mores, politics or religious preferences, but even Celia Randolph had her limits. Elizabeth was well aware that being stood up ranked right up there on her aunt's list of unpardonable social transgressions. "I'm sorry, really. But it was—unavoidable."

"That's another thing," Celia said, regarding her niece suspiciously. "Why won't you tell me why you left, or where you went?"

"It's a long story." In no mood for one of her aunt's third degrees, Elizabeth changed the subject as they entered the elevator. "Who are we dining with anyway?"

"Two couples. I don't think you've met either of them. The Lauers are friends of mine from London and the Contarinis are art dealers from Florence." The elevator came to a stop. "The Contarinis have invited us to spend some time at their villa there after Carnival." She eyed her niece warily as they stepped out. "I suppose I'm in for no end of fuss on that score."

"No fuss. I just can't go. If you'll remember, I'm off to Scotland."

"I assure you Florence is a far more civilized choice this time of year."

"I'll be sure to tell Miss Amore you said so, Celia."

They approached the dining room to find the *copocameriere* guarding his dominion like a well trained watchdog. Fussing over Celia, who was a generous tipper, the headwaiter gathered up two oversized menus and led the pair grandly across the room which, during the ten days of Carnival, took on the festive air of a large Halloween party. Celia had reluctantly given in to Elizabeth's pleas that tonight they eschew costumes for more conventional wear, but she had insisted on dressing up her niece's full-length black dress with a bright Jacquard scarf and gold pin inlaid with precious stones. Elizabeth had steadfastly refused to wear the elaborate matching earrings, however, and had insisted on simply brushing her hair and allowing it to fall freely about her face. If she had to play social butterfly, at least she'd do it dressed in her own clothes and without a head full of pins, powder and fillers.

Since she was walking behind her aunt, Elizabeth didn't see him until they reached the table. Even then it took several moments for her to realize it was really *her* gondolier, calmly sitting there with Celia's friends. As her aunt rattled off the introductions, Elizabeth's fingers gripped the edge of the table in openmouthed shock. It simply could not be!

"And this, Elizabeth, is my dear friend Roberto Roselli," Celia was saying in the triumphant tone of one who has saved the best until last. "I practically had to keep the evening a military secret for fear you'd bolt again, but I've finally managed to get the two of you together.''

Elizabeth's numb mind refused to accept the evidence being transmitted there by her eyes. "You're Roberto Roselli?" She hardly recognized the dry, raspy voice as her own. "*The* Roberto Roselli?"

"I must plead guilty, *signorina*," he said, his voice, his manner, faultlessly polite. Not one iota of recognition showed on the lean, elegant face. "It is indeed a pleasure to meet you at last. I must say that Celia has been far too modest in praising her lovely niece."

Elizabeth swallowed hard. From his head of dark, fashionably-cut hair to the impeccable lines of his expensively-tailored tuxedo, he was every inch the continental gentleman. The very idea that she could have mistaken him for anything less seemed suddenly ludicrous. Only a betraying glint of humor hidden behind the mask of propriety hinted at last night. That merely fed her growing anger. He had lied to her, coolly and deliberately. What easy prey she had been; naive Little Miss Nobody from Smalltown U.S.A. Hardly a match for the man who had been voted Europe's Most Eligible Bachelor three years running.

"Elizabeth, what's the matter with you? I'm sure the gentlemen would be more comfortable eating their dinners sitting down."

Celia's voice brought Elizabeth out of her daze to find that the men were still standing. Forcing what she hoped was a smile onto her face she sank into the chair, keeping her eyes well away from the man who had taught her more about passion in the past twenty-four hours than she had learned in the previous twenty-five years.

As she picked at her food her mind was racing, remembering everything that had passed between them: her candid, unwitting criticisms of Roselli, their intimate conversation in the bell tower. The way she had let him hold her in his arms, kiss her, touch her! Good Lord! By the time dessert arrived her initial shock had turned into a smoldering, white-hot fury, and she had planned her escape. The moment the interminable meal was over she would plead a headache, go to her room and lock the door very firmly behind her.

Foolish thought. Naturally Celia had different ideas. When Elizabeth tried to make her excuses Celia, determined that nothing was going to spoil a party she had gone to such lengths to arrange, slipped Elizabeth two aspirin. Ignoring her niece's glowering looks, she firmly herded everyone to La Fenice, Venice's eighteenth-century opera house, for a performance of Verdi's *La Traviata*.

Under gilded ceilings, the theater wore its most sparkling Carnival finery, but Elizabeth was too agitated to notice. Roberto hadn't approached her since dinner, but every time she sensed his eyes on her she derived some small measure of revenge by coldly ignoring him.

When the lobby lights blinked, signaling the beginning of the performance, Celia hustled them to the second tier of box seats. Assuming their party would divide and share two booths, Elizabeth was taken aback to find that she and Roberto had been deserted. The remaining two seats in their box remained empty; her aunt and her friends were nowhere in sight. Obviously Celia knew a few disappearing tricks of her own.

"You might as well relax and accept it," Roberto said, smiling ruefully. "It appears the bully has struck again."

"With your help, no doubt," she said tightly.

"I've rarely known Celia Randolph to need help." Amusement edged his dulcet voice. "But if it makes you feel any better, I'm as much a victim as you are. I had no idea what she was up to."

"I'll bet you didn't, Carlo."

His smile reminded her of a little boy caught with his hand in the cookie jar. "My middle name," he said a bit sheepishly. "Although it really was the one my mother favored."

"And you knew I'd recognize your first name. Admit it, Signor Roselli. It was a deliberate deception."

His expression became more serious, although the underlying amusement didn't quite leave his face. "As you wish, *signorina*."

"What I really wish is that I'd never met you. Now will you please leave me alone? I've nothing more to say to you."

"Because you're disappointed I'm not a gondolier, or because I'm a disreputable gigolo who feeds on women?"

How like him to dredge all of that up again. "I'd had too much champagne," she retorted, looking at the stage.

"Agreed."

"And I didn't know who you were."

"Obviously."

"And for all I know you probably *do* feed on women!"

"Only for dinner. The rest of the day I'm too busy starving the servants and beating innocent children."

"That's not what I—"

"And don't forget cruelty to animals. One of my favorite pastimes."

"You're being absurd."

"Am I? Then why are you looking at me as if I were a cross between Jack the Ripper and Genghis Khan?"

"I'm not looking at you at all." Hurriedly she fixed her eyes back on the stage. "I told you, I don't want to talk about it." Angry that he had once again bettered her, Elizabeth twisted away from him in her chair. With a grand show of indifference, she turned her attention to the program.

"I didn't realize you read Italian."

She was startled to find him looking over her shoulder, his hand draped lightly on her arm. Gazing down at the program she realized she'd opened it to a section written entirely in Italian. Flustered, she flipped the pages to the English translation and buried her face in the print.

"Have you ever seen *La Traviata*?" he asked.

A muffled "no" emerged from the depths of the program.

His chuckle invaded her system like vintage wine. "Then you are in for a rare treat," he went on in his beautiful voice. "No one performs Verdi like the Venetians."

The opera could have been performed by the Beach Boys for all Elizabeth noticed. Vaguely she realized the staging and costumes were lavish, but if anyone had asked her to describe the libretto she would have been at a loss. Every one of her senses was finely tuned to the man sitting next to her. The very air she breathed seemed charged with his presence. She tried to attribute the erratic state of her nerves to residual anger, but that did not explain why she kept wishing he'd lean over and put his arm around her shoulder. It was madness, pure and simple. Clearly she had slipped a few gears.

By the time intermission arrived she had reached the end of her emotional tether. Slipping out of the box before the last vibrating notes ended the first act she hurried to the lobby, anxious to get away from the whole crazy situation. She had almost reached the entrance when she heard her aunt's unmistakable contralto behind her: "Don't even think about it."

With a resigned sigh, she turned. "I should have known I couldn't escape that easily. How did you get here so fast?"

"I saw you run out of your box as if the devil himself were after you." Since Celia seemed a bit breathless herself, Elizabeth deduced she'd done some running of her own. "I must say I'm very disappointed with you," her aunt went on, fanning herself with a copy of the program. "You didn't speak one word to Roberto during the entire first half of the performance. It was almost as if you were deliberately ignoring him. After all I went through to bring you together."

Elizabeth took a moment to wonder where her aunt had been sitting that she'd been able to keep such a close eye on them. Then she realized Celia had probably had her opera glasses trained on their box from the opening aria. "You should have saved the effort, Celia. I told you I wasn't interested in meeting a man."

"Roberto Roselli can hardly be classified as just *any* man, Elizabeth. There's not a woman in this theater, in Venice for that matter, who wouldn't happily trade places with you."

"Fine. Let them. I'm going back to the hotel."

At this obvious display of dementia, her aunt lost what little was left of her patience. "Don't you dare step a foot outside that door, Elizabeth Bradshaw," she warned, waving her program threateningly. "You're going to see this evening through if I have to tie you to your seat."

"I don't think that will be necessary, Celia," a low voice interrupted. "I'm sure we can find less drastic means to induce your lovely niece to remain."

Elizabeth's heart sank. Of course, who else? In her most cutting tone she turned and said, "Celia has informed me that every woman in Venice is panting to meet you, Signor Roselli. So why don't you run off and make some lady's day."

"Elizabeth!"

"You needn't look so horrified, Celia. Roberto Roselli is very good at sweeping women off their feet. Aren't you, *signore*?"

"Elizabeth Bradshaw, what's gotten into you? I've never known you to be rude like this."

Elizabeth felt Roberto's hand on her arm. Of the three of them, his was the only calm voice. "It's all right, Celia. Elizabeth and I had a small disagreement. Given a few minutes alone I'm sure we can settle our differences." His smile produced its usual devastating effect: Celia melted.

"A lover's spat. Of course, that explains it. You *do* work fast, don't you, Roberto?" She patted his arm, winking conspiratorially. "Off you go then, you two. I almost envy you. There's nothing nicer than making up after a quarrel."

"Oh, great," Elizabeth said, as Celia floated off to join her friends at the bar. "A lover's spat. I'll never live it down."

She started to turn away from him but he took hold of her wrist. His look was serious. "If I've hurt you I'm sorry, Elizabeth. But don't you think you're overreacting just a bit? After all, the initial mistake was yours. You were the one who assumed I was a legitimate gondolier."

"It was a mistake all right," she said, pulling her wrist free. "One you certainly used to full advantage."

"Perhaps so." His look softened. "But the temptation was irresistible. You are a very lovely woman."

"Oh really," she said, her voice heavy with sarcasm. "And that excuses everything, I suppose. Signor Roselli sees, he wants, he takes. And if he tramples a few toes along the way, well, *c'est la vie*."

"It was not that way at all," he said, beginning to lose patience with her. "At the time it seemed harmless enough to go along with the misunderstanding. I didn't realize you would take offense. Obviously I misjudged you."

"Obviously."

"You really do have a tendency to take life too seriously, Elizabeth. The situation is not without its humor."

"That depends on your point of view," she said dryly. "You've probably noticed I'm not laughing."

"Then perhaps it is time that you did. If you continue to close yourself off like this you may awaken one morning to discover that life has passed you by."

"Spare me the advice, I get more than enough from Celia." She looked up at him angrily, at the face she'd seen displayed in so many popular magazines and papers across Europe, and found it difficult to believe they were having this conversation. He'd had his fun with her, now he should be heading for greener, easier pastures. Celia was right, he could have his pick of some of the most beautiful women in the world. Why did he continue to waste time with her?

"You're right about one thing, Roberto," she went on, feeling suddenly drained of emotion. "I'm no good at these games. I don't suppose I'll ever be. So why don't you run off and find someone else to play with? Someone who knows the rules."

With a soft murmur in Italian he reached for her hand, running his thumb lightly over her palm. He did not miss her slight, involuntary shudder as she looked up at him with wary eyes. This time when she tried to pull her hand away, he kept it tightly in his own. "You speak nonsense, Elizabeth," he told her, his voice edged with exasperation. "Can't you see that it is you I care about? I want to show you the excitement you are missing, *mia perla*. I want you to see how good it can be between us."

Desperately she tried to hold on to her anger as every tissue in her body melted in response to his touch. This was not what she had planned. Since dinner she'd thought of little else but giving Roberto Roselli a whopping good piece of her mind. Now, for reasons that defied logical explanation, he was making her feel all soft inside again. You must have the backbone of an amoeba, she thought in self-disgust. This time it wasn't going to work. For once in his pampered life, Roberto Roselli was going to hear the word no.

"You seem to be laboring under a misconception, *signore*," she told him in cool, flat tones. "I already have all the excitement I want in my life. And difficult as it may be for you to believe, not every woman you meet is pining for a chance to jump into bed with you.''

As if to put the lie to her words, a beautiful ash blonde waved at Roberto and snaked her way over. Tall and willowy, her model-thin figure was draped in a sleek creation of black-and-gold metallic. She flashed a dazzling smile and sang out in a thin soprano, ''Roberto, where have you been? We've been looking everywhere for you.''

''I see you've found him, Nina,'' said a lower, more controlled voice, watching as Roberto placed a kiss on the blonde's rouged cheek. The newcomer was a stunning brunette with flashing hazel eyes and a traffic-stopping figure. She gave Roberto a reproving look. ''How naughty of you to avoid us, darling. We thought you'd decided not to do Verdi tonight after all.''

More people joined the group, the majority of them women, most of them chic and lovely. Although she had never considered herself vain, Elizabeth couldn't help feeling underdressed and awkward in such fashionable company. Her classic black outfit, so stylish in Wheat Ridge, seemed a continent removed from the flashy St. Laurents and the smart Diors. Judging by the surreptitious looks aimed in her direction, Elizabeth decided she wasn't alone in this assessment.

When the usual rush of small talk was exhausted, the conversation inevitably came around to Diavolo, Roberto's champion racer, and the upcoming Verona Stakes scheduled to be run the following week. Since she'd done some research on the European racing circuit, Elizabeth knew this was one of Italy's *prima* racing events of the year. When she innocently admitted she'd never set foot on a race track, however, Roberto's friends seemed scandalized.

''Never been to a horse race?'' The blonde was looking at Elizabeth as if she'd just confessed to being a hatchet murderer. ''You're not serious.''

"Wherever did you find her, darling?" asked the brunette in a tone that made Elizabeth feel like an interesting bug the woman had unearthed from beneath a rock. There was a general titter of laughter and Elizabeth silently bristled. "Obviously Roberto's been keeping secrets from us," the brunette went on, implying that Elizabeth was one secret that would have been better left unshared.

"You'll have to bring her to Verona," said a tall man dressed as an eighteenth-century French dandy. "I'll be happy to enlighten this pretty young innocent on the intricacies of pari-mutuel betting."

"You mean pari-mutuel *losing*, don't you, George?" another man put in. "I haven't seen you win a wager all year."

Another wave of laughter. "Pretty young innocent"! Elizabeth felt the small hairs rising on the back of her neck.

"The way Roberto's holding on to her she doesn't have to know anything about racing," the second man said, looking Elizabeth up and down appraisingly. "Did I hear you say she's a librarian?"

"A librarian! Darling, you're joking." The blonde's heavily kohled eyes flew to Elizabeth as she assessed this remarkable piece of information. "She doesn't look like a librarian." A giggle. "I mean all the librarians I've known have had their hair in buns and worn horn-rimmed glasses. Anyway, the last place I'd expect to find Roberto is in a library."

Silently, Elizabeth fumed. The blonde made library sound like a dirty word! And why did they keep talking about her as if she weren't there—or didn't have the brains to follow the conversation? Even if she hadn't been raised in the sophisticated world of the jet-setter, she'd learned better manners than this by the third grade.

When the French dandy asked Roberto if he planned to broaden Elizabeth's horizons by bringing her to Verona to see the "sport of kings," Elizabeth had finally had enough.

If she hadn't been so put out with Celia for forcing all of this on her in the first place or angry with Roberto for stirring up emotions better left dormant, she might have found the patience to swallow her pride and keep peace. But too much had happened to her over the past two days. Something inside Elizabeth snapped.

"No, he won't be taking her to Verona," she said, pasting a fulsome smile on her face. "The little librarian regrets she will be too busy cleaning her glasses and dusting her books to attend. You all know what books are, don't you?" she said, beaming innocently at the blonde. "Sheets of printed paper fastened together and placed between protective covers? They contain all sorts of fascinating information, such as Joseph Oller's method of pari-mutuel betting, which—" this to the dandy "—you might find profitable reading. Also, you might be interested in the history of the Verona Stakes which since its establishment in 1831 and has gone on to become, after the Prix de l'Arc de Triomphe and the Grand Prix de Paris, one of continental Europe's most impressive racing events. Riolet, if you'll recall, had his greatest triumph there against Chiaro in 1932."

She flashed a dazzling smile. "Now if you'll excuse me, everyone, I think the second act is about to begin."

Five

For someone who's never been to a horse race, you seem to know a great deal about the sport.''

It was nearing midnight, and now that they were finally away from an annoying clique of society reporters who'd been hovering outside the opera house with cameras flashing, Elizabeth found herself actually enjoying the walk back to her hotel. The magic of Carnival seemed even more compelling this close to the witching hour. All around them the city was bathed in crystalline hues, the narrow streets and bridges transformed into a whimsical world of lights and color and noise. In the distance a fireworks display lit the sky reminding Elizabeth of a childhood trip to Disneyland, and sounds of laughter and singing came to them from every street corner and piazza.

For reasons known best to herself, Celia had been nowhere in sight at the end of the performance. But if this vanishing act had been a not-so-subtle ploy to nudge her

niece into Roberto's arms, Elizabeth was equally determined that it wouldn't work. She'd had the last two acts of
La Traviata to steel herself against him. Last night she'd
been taken unaware. Tonight she would be in control if it
killed her.

"It was because of *Passion's Play*," she said, concentrating on keeping a respectable distance between them as
they walked. "The reason I knew about horse racing, I
mean."

"*Passion's Play*? No, don't tell me. Another book by
Venus Amore."

She nodded, relieved the conversation was staying on safe
ground. "Her fourth. The hero, Pierre Dubois, is a French
horse breeder. Once I got into the research, I found the history of horse racing fascinating. Did you know there's evidence that the Hittites were breeding and training horses for
racing as early as the fifteenth century B.C.?"

"Amazing." He smiled down at her just as her face was
lit by another explosion of fireworks. "And you store all this
information in your mind like a computer?"

"I have a good memory. It comes in handy for my work."

"Or for putting people in their place?"

She stole a quick glance at him. It was the first mention
he'd made of her outburst since she'd stormed back to her
seat after intermission. "I lost my temper," she muttered,
looking away.

"You don't approve of my friends, do you, Elizabeth?"

She hesitated a moment before answering, reluctant to
provoke another argument. "People like that bother me.
They remind me of a movie set, all false fronts with nothing inside. I always have the feeling that they're talking to
create an impression, not because of a personal conviction
or idea."

"And you are a woman of strong convictions, aren't
you?" He studied her profile in the moonlight, admiring the

pure, soft lines and the determined set of her small chin, then tried to imagine his friends from her point of view. "I can see how you might find them a bit frivolous. Although I assure you that in their own right most of them are quite accomplished."

Elizabeth was tempted to ask if he was referring to their accomplished ability to lose money at the track or to choose designer clothing, but decided she'd said enough for one night.

They were silent again as they walked along the Mercerie, its shop windows displaying plastic gondolas and blown glass from the island of Murano. Above their heads pots of flowers dangled from a balcony to belie the fact that spring would not officially arrive in Venice for some weeks yet. Although he made no move to cross the invisible line she had drawn between them, Elizabeth was intensely aware of his presence beside her. Some people just seemed to be born with an inordinate amount of charisma, she decided. Was that why she, who had always considered herself so practical and down-to-earth, was having such a difficult time resisting him?

"You're still angry with me, aren't you?"

His tone was light, yet some part of her recognized his subtle anxiety to know. Which raised other interesting questions, such as why he should care one wit whether she was angry with him or not. Maybe he was just one of those men whose ego demanded that every woman he meet fall adoringly at his feet. Was that the flip side of being born with such charisma?

"I'd say I have good reason to be angry," she said evenly.

"But I have apologized. It was never my intention to hurt you, Elizabeth. Why do you find it so difficult to forgive?"

She searched his face as they walked, looking for signs that he was putting her on again. All she could detect was a kind of sober intensity and a fleeting glimpse of something else that she couldn't identify. "I imagine you're used to having women forgive you when you behave abominably. Does anyone ever say no to you, Roberto?"

"Occasionally." He paused and his eyes lit with mischief. "Perhaps I would have been more inclined to admit my true identity if you hadn't already decided Roberto Roselli was such a *giocatore*, a gigolo."

"Your reputation precedes you, Signor Roselli. Pick up any newspaper and read about yourself sometime."

"As a researcher you should know you cannot believe everything you read."

"Perhaps not. But where there's smoke—" They had reached her hotel and she broke off, relieved that the uncomfortable evening was almost over. "Thank you for walking me home, Signor Roselli. There's no need to see me inside."

He reached for her hand before she could slip into the lobby. Once again her stomach did a disconcerting flip-flop at his touch, and she could not seem to control the sudden heat that rushed to her cheeks. Has he bewitched me, she wondered, or is it simply the spell of Carnival, of Venice?

"This afternoon you admitted being afraid of men, Elizabeth," he said softly, cradling her hand gently between his palms. "Believe me, the last thing I want to do is add to your apprehension. I would only like to show you what is missing from your life. I want you to see how exciting and wonderful it could be between us."

The hidden arrogance in these quiet words took several moments to pierce Elizabeth's senses. *He* would fix her life, make it exciting and wonderful. Providing, of course, that she consented to go to bed with him. How very like the Roberto Rosellis of this world to think they had the power to make a woman complete and fulfilled.

"Don't you consider it a bit presumptive to assume you know what's missing from my life?" she said, beginning to bristle. "How can you possibly understand what I feel?"

"But that's part of the problem, Elizabeth, isn't it? You are afraid to allow yourself to feel. If you open yourself to love and passion, you might have to experience pain as well, and it's just not worth the risk."

She drew back from him, all the more disturbed by what he was saying because she knew it contained a grain of truth. "Fortunately what I'm willing to risk isn't your problem, Signor Roselli," she said, trying to snub him but merely succeeding in sounding shaky. "Now, if you'll excuse me, I'll say good night—and goodbye."

Before she could turn he pulled her abruptly into his arms. He could feel the rapid beat of her heart against his chest as her expressive eyes blazed up at him. Probing them he saw resentment and fear. He also saw the mirror reflection of his own desire.

"I've felt the hunger you try so hard to suppress, Elizabeth. Beneath that cool, practical facade a passionate woman is struggling to emerge. Oh, no!" He halted her attempt to pull away. "Hear me out. Who are you really afraid of, Elizabeth? Are you quite sure that it is me, or could it be yourself? Are you that frightened of what might happen if, just once, you let yourself go?"

"Yes, I'm afraid," she blurted, too upset now to care how much she revealed. "And with good reason. I've seen what can happen when passion takes precedence over reason. I don't want that kind of chaos in my life. I can't—I can't handle it."

He lifted her chin with his finger and saw the tears welling in her eyes. For a moment she was painfully open, her defenses exposed and vulnerable. He wanted to take her in his arms and reassure her that everything would be all right, that he could never hurt her, but his desire for her was so strong that he was afraid of holding her too close.

"Elizabeth, darling—why does it have to be chaotic? Believe me there is nothing more beautiful, more precious, than love between a man and a woman. You are missing so much, *mia bella*." His next words were a warm whisper against her mouth. "Let me show you how beautiful it can be."

Of their own accord her lips trembled apart at his touch. At first his lips were firm but gentle, as if he were wary of frightening her away. Then, one aching degree at a time, he deepened the kiss until Elizabeth's legs weakened and she knew she was hopelessly ensnared.

One arm held her around the waist, the other moved to the back of her neck to tilt her head as he changed the nature of the embrace. He murmured something she didn't quite catch, then she shuddered as his lips became persuasive, ardently seductive. Against her will, hating herself even as she succumbed, she melted into his strong, waiting body.

Passion rose like a giant wave, engulfing her from the tips of her toes to the top of her whirling head. All her arguments were lost beneath the urgent exploration of his talented hands and the hot, fevered thrust of his tongue against hers. As he molded her even more tightly against his lean hardness she felt his desire for her, and it struck a triumphant, answering response in her own body. Her numbed mind tried to make sense of her churning emotions, but logical thought had become impossible. She had never felt anything this intensely, never in her life had she needed a man so desperately. Her whole being was finely tuned to him, only him.

When he finally released her she drew in deep gulps of air, fighting to hang on to the last fragile threads of control. His hands came up to frame her face, tilting up her head until he could look deep into her eyes.

"Intellectually you may deny your emotions," he said, his voice uneven. "But your body does not lie. I can feel it tremble beneath my fingers when I touch you. There is so much there, little one, so very much." He drew in a deep, betraying breath. "I want to be the man to awaken all that passion in you, *mia perla*. I want to show you what it is like to love."

She pushed away from him, fighting to regain her slipping control. His words stung her mind even as they sent her emotions into a tailspin. She tried to sort through her feelings, to identify and separate and confront them, but they were too strange and unfamiliar. And he was too distracting. She needed time to acknowledge and understand a part of herself she had scarcely known existed before now. "And if I choose not to know? Will you go away and leave me in peace?"

He searched her eyes, holding her captive with his mesmeric gaze. "Is that what you want, Elizabeth? Are you quite sure?"

She paused, unable for a moment to break the invisible thread that bound her to him. This is it, she thought, willing herself to be strong. He's giving you the chance to break away from this madness. For God's sake, take it!

"Yes, that's what I want." She tried to smile, but a single, traitorous tear ruined the effect. "I think it's best for both of us if we go back to our own worlds." Before you hurt me, she added silently. Because I know if I don't break this thing off here and now the day will come when you will hurt me.

He continued to look at her for a long, thoughtful moment, then, using the back of his forefinger, gently brushed away the moisture from her cheek. "I'm not sure you know what you want."

Through the darkness she sensed his smile as he bent down and kissed her lightly on the lips. "For now I will just say good night, Elizabeth," he told her softly. "I do not think either of us is ready as yet to say goodbye."

The first of the flowers—two dozen blood-red carnations—was delivered before breakfast the next morning. The enclosed card, written in a strong, deliberate hand, read: "From my heart to yours. May they soon beat as one." A postscript added to the bottom of the card said, "From Venus Amore's first book, *Sweet Savage Surrender*."

The second delivery, a brilliant display of chrysanthemums in yellow, white, red, purple and blue, arrived in time for lunch with a card imploring Elizabeth to: "Let me light up your life."

That afternoon, the porter, his dark, rakish face grinning in ill-concealed curiosity, deposited a lavish display of Canterbury bells and a card that said: "I want to set your heart ringing."

When the arrangement of yellow roses and dainty violets arrived after tea, Celia beat Elizabeth to the door. Without waiting for an invitation, she flipped open the enclosed card with one long, ruby-painted nail and read: "'Roses are red, violets are blue. Join me this evening in dinner for two.'"

Celia chuckled appreciatively. "Well, I must say Byron has nothing to worry about. But it's the thought that counts." She eyed her niece challengingly. "You're going of course."

"I'm doing no such thing." Elizabeth took the card and sent it fluttering down to join its predecessors in the wastebasket, then looked around the sitting room in distaste. "This place is beginning to smell like a funeral parlor."

"You're hopeless, did you know that? There's not a woman alive who could resist these flowers." Celia swept a dramatic arm around the room. "*Or* Roberto."

"I can, Celia. I haven't spent the past ten years planning out my future just to throw it all away because Roberto Roselli's decided he wants a little Carnival fling." She stormed off toward the bedroom. "I'm ordering dinner from room service tonight. If any more flowers arrive you have my blessing to burn them!"

The candy, ten pounds of assorted chocolates, nuts and chews, arrived with the dessert tray, and an hour later the intrigued porter delivered a beautifully wrapped package that made the first serious dent in Elizabeth's defenses. Opening the paper, she was astonished to find herself holding an exquisite first edition written by eighteenth-century philosopher and legal theorist, Jeremy Bentham. His famous treatise, *Principles of Morals and Legislation*, had been published in 1789.

The porter waited patiently, this course of action having previously rewarded him with ten pounds of candy and enough flowers to court half the maids at the hotel. But Elizabeth had forgotten he was there. Running her fingers lovingly over the faded red cover, the delicate, beautifully preserved pages, she simply couldn't bring herself to callously consign Bentham's masterpiece to the same fate as the flowers and candy. A treasure like this happened along once in a lifetime, if then. Even if Mephistopheles himself had sent the book, she knew she'd have been powerless to refuse.

With trembling fingers she opened the accompanying card and read: "Meet me for a nightcap and we can discuss eighteenth-century mores. An in-depth, hands-on examination of these principles to follow if you're so inclined."

The porter gave a polite little cough. "The gentleman said there would be a reply, *signorina*," he said expectantly.

"No," she answered, somewhat surprised to see him still standing there. "No reply." She fumbled in her purse for a tip, then closed the door in the porter's crestfallen face.

After he left she stood staring at the book as if it were some kind of poisonous reptile. She should have sent it

back, she told herself. At the very least she should have
thanked Roberto. But that would have meant sending him
a message, and right now that was the one thing she was incapable of doing. How could she make any sort of sensible
reply when she was torn apart by a desire to see him and the
belief that seeing him again would be the height of insanity?

When the musicians began playing in the street beneath
her window, Elizabeth had finally fallen into a restless sleep
after hours of pacing and countless lectures to herself on the
dangers of men like Roselli who came bearing gifts, especially gifts as valuable as rare first editions. At first the
violins provided a soothing backdrop to her troubled
dreams, but when the strings were joined by a loud, vibrating tenor, she sat bolt upright in her bed.

Fumbling her way to the partially open window, she
pulled back the curtain to find four men standing in a semi-
circle below her second-floor window, three violinists posi-
tioned behind the portly tenor. It was a dazed moment or
two before Elizabeth realized *she* was the object of the serenade. Several other guests, she noted in acute embarrassment, had made the discovery at roughly the same time.

"Psst," she hissed down to the musicians. "Go away.
It's—" She squinted at her glow-in-the-dark travel clock.
Good Lord! It was after one. "Go away. Sing somewhere
else."

At her voice a fifth figure emerged from the shadows, his
tall, lean form unmistakable. Roberto! Of course, she
should have guessed. "Why are you doing this to me?" she
called down to him in a hoarse whisper.

"You did not answer my note," he said simply. "The
florist is closed for the night and so is the confectionery.
And when even Bentham couldn't pierce your heart,
well..." Through the moonlight she could see his face crease

into a slow, easy grin as he spread his arms in a gesture of defeat. "What else could I do but come myself?"

"What else?" If there had been a flowerpot handy she'd have happily dropped it on his head to show him what else he could have done. "Why can't you accept the fact that I don't want to see you again? Go pester your blond friend, Nina, or the curvy brunette who fawned all over you last night. They looked as if they'd be more than eager to explore eighteenth-century mores with you."

"But I don't want to explore it with them. You are the expert."

"Not for what you have in mind," she said, wishing the musicians would stop looking up at her so lasciviously. Someone from an adjoining room yelled at her to give the guy a break so they could all get some sleep, and she lowered her voice to an angry whisper. "Go away. You're disturbing the other guests."

"And you are disturbing me," he replied, not bothering to be quiet. "I will not leave until you agree to see me tomorrow."

"You pulled that trick in the bell tower yesterday. I'm not falling for it twice."

"Ah, well," he sighed. "If that is your final word." He turned to the musicians. "Gentlemen, if you would be so kind."

The night air was once again pierced by violins, this time the musicians striking up a lively aria that the tenor entered into with uninhibited gusto. Elizabeth heard more windows bang open, while their occupants vented their displeasure with angry shouts and dire threats. "Will you please go away," she pleaded above the racket.

"Only if you will agree to see me tomorrow," he replied, serenely surveying the bedlam with folded arms.

"You're despicable!"

"And you are particularly delectable in dishabille," he replied, thoughtfully eyeing her décolletage.

Elizabeth looked down at the low-cut bodice of her nightgown, supplied of course by Celia, ostensively to replace the ones her aunt had "misplaced" while helping Elizabeth to unpack. Too late she realized she'd run to the window without pulling on the matching robe. Shrinking back, she clutched her hands over her exposed cleavage. "This time you've gone too far, Roselli," she cried, no longer caring if all of Venice heard her. "You're a—a first-class cad."

Roberto shrugged good-naturedly. "A bit archaic, perhaps, but I've been called worse." He smiled that sexy, heart-stopping grin that did such disastrous things to her pulse rate and went on, as calmly as if he'd called to invite her to the school prom, "Well, will you go out with me tomorrow?"

A chorus of shouts from unhappy hotel guests suggested in varying degrees of rudeness that she accept his offer. Realizing he would never leave unless she agreed, she said, "You're worse than a cad. You're—you're lower than a worm. Yes, blast it, I'll go out with you. It's either that or get lynched by my neighbors. But only if you promise it will be in neutral territory, out in the open where there'll be no opportunity for hanky-panky."

"Elizabeth." He looked crushed that she would suggest such a thing. "Do you really think I would stoop to anything as ungallant as—hanky-panky?" He smiled up at the sea of angry faces hanging out of the windows as if seeking confirmation that this was indeed a villainous accusation. Whether out of a desire to shut him up or because they were beginning to sympathize with his cause, the faces came out loudly in his defense, a decision so popular with the musicians that they promptly struck up a rousing scherzo with the tenor slapping time with a tambourine.

"You don't know the meaning of the word gallant," she shouted, trying to make herself heard above the clamor. "Take it or leave it, Roselli. Those are my terms."

He performed a mock little bow, indicating at the same time that his musicians could stop playing. "I am moved by your gracious acceptance, *signorina*. I'll pick you up tomorrow morning at seven. Oh, and dress comfortably—and warm," he added as an afterthought.

To the mingled catcalls and cheers of the other tenants, he waved his hand cheerily and walked off, his exuberant string quartet following close behind. Elizabeth watched him with gritted teeth, then realizing she was still very much the center of attention, hurriedly drew in her head and slammed the window closed behind her.

The following day dawned crisp and clear, a miracle, Celia informed her as she watched her niece's desultory preparations. Three consecutive February days in Venice without rain was an unheard-of luxury.

"Clearly it's meant as a good omen," she went on, a bit put off by her niece's refusal to impart any but the most perfunctory information about her date. "Did Roberto say where he was taking you?"

A negative grunt as Elizabeth pulled on her poking-about-the-countryside boots.

"Surely you're not going to wear those old things?" Celia said, horrified.

"He said to dress warm and comfortably," Elizabeth muttered. "I am."

"I assure you, Elizabeth, there are any number of attractive ways to keep warm. Those shoes are most assuredly not one of them. And darling, must you wear jeans?"

Elizabeth was secretly gratified to see what it cost her aunt to even speak the odious word. To Celia Randolph, jeans were only slightly less abhorrent than hard rock music as a modern social plague. To make it worse, Elizabeth's didn't even sport a designer label to distinguish them from their peers. They were simply nameless, off the rack, comfortable.

But if she'd expected a negative response from Roberto concerning her choice of clothes, she was disappointed. In fact, his sweater and denim pants very nearly matched her own, except that she detected an exclusive label on his hip pocket when he leaned over to help her into the water taxi.

"I don't suppose you thought to wear thermal underwear," he commented once they were settled in the boat. At her startled look he went on, "Never mind. I'm sure Marina will have some that fit. And I've asked her to bring along more suitable pants for us as well."

"Marina?" A picture of one of Roberto's beautiful women flashed into her mind. She had a sudden, disturbing mental image of—a ménage à trois, wasn't that what they called it? Dear Lord, what had she let herself in for?

"And of course we can rent the rest of the equipment when we get there," he went on, oblivious to her growing panic.

Equipment! Sordid images crowded her fevered brain. She searched through the files in her mind for stories she'd read describing the wild parties enjoyed by the idle rich. She'd heard that jet-setters frequently took a casual view of sex. Was that the sort of day he had in mind?

Slowly, carefully, she inched as far away from him on the seat as possible. Elizabeth, you have got to get out of here, she told herself, remembering that keeping a cool head was the first, most imperative line of defense. But the moment the taxi docked she would run, not walk, away from him.

She stumbled in her haste to disembark, and Roberto reached out a strong arm to help her ashore, an arm he showed no inclination to withdraw once they were safely on the street. Instead, he led her down a short flight of stairs to a parking area, the first cars she had seen since her arrival in Venice. Before she could make a break for it, he had settled her in the cushy bucket seat of a bright-red Maserati, instructed her to fasten her seat belt and started the engine. With shaking hands she pulled the belt across her shoulder and fastened the buckle, frightening images of other, more devious holding devices flashing unbidden into her mind. Now what? her inner voice demanded. How do you propose to get out of this one?

Even if she'd wanted to, Elizabeth knew she was incapable of speech as the sportscar roared up the *autostrada*. Her throat was so dry she could barely swallow, much less attempt verbalization. As near as she could figure, they were headed due north, and increasing patches of snow to either side of the *strada* indicated the temperature outside was dropping rapidly. For some time Roberto was quiet as he concentrated on his driving, and when he finally broke the silence her nerves were so taut that she gave a little jump.

"Relax, Elizabeth, enjoy the ride," he said, glancing at her rigid profile. "I think you'll like my friends. They're a good deal more free and easy than the crowd you met at the opera. Very informal."

Friends. Plural! Beneath her stiff exterior Elizabeth's mind was racing. These friends—Marina and God only knew how many others—were free and easy. Of course, they'd have to be for what he had planned. It was worse than a ménage à trois. He was taking her to a full-scale orgy!

"Do we—" She paused, swallowing hard to lubricate her parched throat. "Do we have far to go?"

"Not too far. But toward the end the road becomes narrow and very windy. It can be slow going, especially in the winter. Selva Gardena is located near the Austrian border."

Selva Gardena. The name was familiar, where had she heard it before? Was it famous—no, infamous—for this kind of activity? Surely there would be a phone there. She could call for help. Celia would know what to do.

As he predicted, the road soon narrowed and Roberto stopped talking to give all his attention to the icy twists and turns. If she hadn't been so busy imagining a seemingly endless variety of unsavory activities, she might have enjoyed the view. Sun glistened on the snow-covered trees to form a winter paradise; the sky, blue and crystal clear, promised a glorious day. To do what, Elizabeth? What lies ahead at Selva Gardena?

The first hint appeared when they passed a row of buildings—old, quaint and styled like Swiss chalets—that pictured skiers on wooden, hand-painted signs hung prominently in front of the shops. For a long moment, Elizabeth's harassed brain refused to compute this new information. Then Roberto stopped the car in front of a shop advertising ski rentals, and the pieces clicked into place with ridiculous, disconcerting simplicity. Thermal underwear, rental equipment, Selva Gardena. Of course she'd heard of it. Selva Gardena was one of the most popular ski resorts on the southern slopes of the Italian Alps.

He isn't taking you to an orgy, you idiot, she told herself in near hysterical relief. He's brought you up here to ski!

Six

You said you wanted to spend the day out in the open."
Roberto smiled at Elizabeth as he carried their skis to the
lodge. "Well, the Alps are about as open as you can get."

"Why didn't you tell me you were taking me skiing?"

"Actually, I thought I had." He put her equipment next
to his in a coin-operated ski rack, pulled the bar across and
locked it in. "You weren't exactly in a talkative mood last
night if you'll remember. But it must have been pretty obvious when I mentioned the thermal underwear and Selva
Gardena. Where did you think we were going?"

She gave a discreet cough. There was no way she was
going to tell him what she thought. "You mentioned we
were meeting some of your friends," she reminded him,
changing the subject.

"Yes, we are. They're probably waiting for us inside."

As they entered the lodge a dark, muscular young man,
not quite as tall as Roberto, gave them a hearty greeting.

Giorgio Baciocco was a former classmate of Roberto's from university days, and judging by the amount of backslapping and explosive, laughing Italian that passed between them, the two had remained close friends.

Giorgio's younger sister Marina, whose name had given Elizabeth so many bad moments in the car, turned out to be a vivacious, pretty woman of about twenty-six, with dark, curly hair and warm, flashing brown eyes. In halting but careful English, she presented Elizabeth with the promised thermals and a pair of black, stretch-style ski pants.

"It was necessary for me to guess your size from Roberto's description," she said with an apologetic smile. "With the thermals, of course, size is of little consequence. But with the pants it is hoped they are a proper fit."

Since the pants turned out to be a perfect fit, Elizabeth was set to wondering how Roberto had so accurately gauged her measurements. Obviously he was no stranger to assessing the female figure, she decided ruefully.

As they waited for the ski lift, Giorgio's brown eyes sparkled with mischief as he complimented Roberto on his excellent choice of a companion. "If your skiing is half as breathtaking as your beauty, I look forward to watching you on the slopes," he told Elizabeth with a broad, good-natured smile.

"I don't know about the breathtaking part," she said, embarrassed but pleased with the compliment. "But I was born with the Rocky Mountains in my backyard. My friends and I knew how to ski before we could walk."

When they came off the ski lift, Elizabeth caught her breath at the spectacular vista spread out below. "I thought the Rockies were the most picturesque mountains in the world," she said in quiet wonder. "Now, after seeing this, I'm not so sure."

"It never fails to move me as well," Marina said, looking out over the glacially etched valleys, the sharp, narrow mountain crests, the glistening snow. "Like you I have lived in the shadow of the mountains all my life." Her clear, bubbling laughter infected them all. "We are lucky, the four of us, are we not?"

Elizabeth caught Roberto looking at her, his face wearing that same, enigmatic expression she'd noticed when they walked back from the opera. Then he smiled and she was inexplicably filled with a heady sense of well-being. Suddenly she couldn't wait to attack the hill. "Come on," she called out, pushing off the cornice. "Last one down the slope is a snow bunny!"

The day passed too quickly. Experienced skiers, Marina and Giorgio led them from one run to another; it seemed to Elizabeth they never went on the same lift twice. At the end of each run, Roberto would unfailingly be there beside her. Their skills were so evenly matched that Marina swore their skis barely touched the snow as they flew side by side down the hill.

They all had lunch in one of the resort's chalets located midway up the mountain, and the bottle of *barbera* Giorgio bought to go with their pizza added a pleasant glow to the meal. At the end of the day they drank steaming cups of cappuccino in front of the main lodge's fireplace, laughing as they recounted the day's adventures.

When the time finally came to say goodbye, Elizabeth felt as if Marina and Giorgio were old friends. Later, while riding back in the car, she found herself comparing them with the crowd she'd met at La Fenice two nights ago. It was amazing, she thought, that Roberto could have such diverse friends, almost as if he were two different people. Thinking about this during the drive back to Venice, she decided she liked today's Roberto much better than the tuxedo-clad jet-setter whose friends were more concerned with being seen than being themselves. But which man was the real Roselli? Yawning, she wondered drowsily if she'd ever know the answer.

Elizabeth awoke, disoriented, to find it had grown very dark. It was several minutes before she realized they had left the mountains and the main road and were bumping along a narrow country lane. "This isn't the way we came," she said, bolting upright.

"I know. I want to show you something before we go back to the city."

"What kind of something?" She repressed the outrageous, but not totally unappealing idea, that he was kidnapping her, sweeping her off to some secluded trysting place where he would proceed to make mad, passionate love to her. Good grief, Elizabeth, she told herself with a mental shake. You're beginning to sound like one of Miss Amore's heroines. Haven't you done enough fantasizing for one day? Still, she wondered, why had he turned off the main road and what did he want to show her?

He smiled mysteriously and maneuvered the car smoothly through impressive wrought-iron gates. "You will see in a few minutes. We're almost there."

Pressing her nose against the window, she saw they were passing what looked like a large meadow. Since the moon had not yet fully risen, she could just make out several dark shadows moving between the trees, and one or two that were stationary. Of course, she thought, they were horses.

"This is your ranch, isn't it, Roberto?" she said, turning to look at him. "But where are we? I mean in relationship to Venice?"

"We're in Feltre, about forty miles north of Venice. Verona is approximately the same distance southeast as the crow flies." He pulled up in front of a three-storied mansion, stone gray and massive, which bore little resemblance to Elizabeth's idea of a ranch house.

"It's very—impressive," she said, not knowing quite how to put her reaction into words.

"What you mean is it doesn't look much like a ranch. By American standards, you're right. The original structure dates from the early eighteenth century. In those days a man's wealth was measured as much by the size and grandeur of his house as it was by the amount of land he owned or his livestock. My ancestors built accordingly." He came around and opened the door. "My great-great-grandfather added two new wings in the 1840s, and there have been frequent remodelings over the years. Since I have little use for sixty-eight rooms, however, I keep most of them closed off. This way," he added, taking her arm.

To her surprise he led her away from the house toward the stables. Elizabeth was curious to note that these structures were far more modern than the house. They entered through a wide breezeway, and a thin, elderly little man with gray hair and a sweeping, old-fashioned mustache, poked his head out of the tack room. He greeted Roberto affectionately in Italian, and after several minutes of animated conversation which, from her limited knowledge of the language seemed to refer exclusively to horses, Roberto brought the old man over to be introduced.

"Tommaso, I want you to meet Signorina Bradshaw. Elizabeth, Tommaso Ciatti. Tommaso is my right hand on the ranch. He's been teaching me everything I know since I was old enough to be propped up in a saddle."

"*Sciocchezza*, nonsense," the man said, clapping Roberto on the back. "This man, he was born on a horse. No need for me or anyone else to teach."

Ignoring the older man's modesty, Roberto went on fondly, "Without Tommaso there probably would be no Roselli Stables today. He's the one who convinced me to invest in Vento Felice, which means fair wind. At the time I practically had to mortgage my life to buy that old stallion, but it was his foal that rebuilt our stock. Fifteen of Vento's offsprings went on to become champions. And of course he's Diavolo's grandsire."

Elizabeth's interest peaked at the mention of the famous thoroughbred. She closed her eyes and mentally ticked off his record: "A Triple Crown win in the Derby, the 2000 Guineas and the St. Leger as a three-year-old established Diavolo as a world-class champion. Last year he had two more impressive wins, the Gold Cup and the Prix de l'Arc Triomphe where he set a new track record. This year he's the odds favorite at the Verona Stakes." Elizabeth opened her eyes to find Roberto and Tommaso regarding her in astonishment. She grinned sheepishly. "I happened to remember from the research I did on—"

"*Passion's Play*," she and Roberto finished together.

"Elizabeth, you are truly amazing." He laughed and took her hand. "Come along then. Since you already know Diavolo's vital statistics, it's time you met him in the flesh. He's quite a character."

Character wasn't quite the adjective Elizabeth would have expected to describe the horse who was well on his way to becoming one of the greatest champions in racing history. When she heard a loud whinny from a stall at the far end of the stable, however, she began to see what Roberto meant. The stallion was shaking his head impatiently as he watched them approach, and if it were possible for a horse to smile, she would have sworn this one did.

"I spent a lot of time with him as a colt and during his early training," Roberto explained, stroking the white diamond that marked the great bay's forehead. Diavolo rubbed his nose against Roberto's shoulder, then blew softly and bent his head to nudge Roberto's pocket. "He's also very spoiled." He laughed and produced a cube of sugar which the stallion eagerly consumed.

Despite the information she'd collected researching Miss Amore's book, Elizabeth knew very little about horses. She did, however, recognize a beautiful animal when she saw one. Diavolo was a truly magnificent creature. Tall for a racer, nearly eighteen-hands high, he was a rich, deep reddish-brown, and every inch of his sleek, muscular body proclaimed his great speed He had a slender neck, a short back, long, narrow legs and bright, intelligent eyes.

As if reading her thoughts Roberto directed the horse to say hello to their visitor. When Diavolo promptly turned to her and whinnied, they both laughed.

"Don't tell me he really understood you," she said, reaching out a tentative hand to stroke the horse's neck. "I didn't realize horses could be trained to do that."

"Shh," he said, winking. "Diavolo thinks *he's* the one who trained me."

Elizabeth looked around the stable. Even though it was late in the day she was surprised that it was so quiet. One of Italy's biggest races of the year was coming up the following week, and she expected the trainers to be working overtime. "I know next week's race is important. Shouldn't Diavolo be training or something?"

"In a sense, the Verona Stakes is Diavolo's most important race so far," he said seriously. "As you pointed out the other evening, it is Italy's principal racing event, and being so close to Feltre it is the nearest thing we have to a home track. It has long been my dream to cap Diavolo's career with a win at Verona." He ran his hand along the animal's neck to his withers, amazed as always by the power that rippled beneath the graceful lines. "But to answer your question, he does train, every morning. I prefer, however, to keep my horses under as little pressure as possible, at least until race time. Then the tension is unavoidable, and probably even beneficial to their performances." Diavolo nuzzled Roberto's cheek, and when he went on Elizabeth could hear the affection in his voice. "You'll be ready, won't you, *mio amico*?"

As if on cue, the horse nodded his head up and down and gave another loud whinny. When they were through laughing, Roberto regarded her seriously. "It would please me very much if you would come with me to see Diavolo run next week, Elizabeth."

The invitation took her by surprise. "I don't know, Roberto. I'll—I'll have to think about it. Oh!" She gave a little jump as Diavolo nuzzled her jacket pocket. When Roberto slipped her a sugar cube, she held out her hand to the horse a bit diffidently.

"Don't be afraid. He won't bite."

"Not like you at Maria Carmagnola's party, huh?"

He laughed. "You do have a remarkable memory. I'm not sure I like that. There are some things I would prefer people to forget."

"Such as?" Looking at Roberto she realized how very little she really knew about him. "You know you've told me almost nothing about yourself, yet you practically know my life's history. Turnabout's fair play, don't you think?"

He looked at her for a moment, then gave the horse a final pat. "All right, but not here. I wouldn't want Diavolo to overhear anything he could use against me later."

They ate dinner in front of a blazing fire in the living room. It was simple food, the kind Roberto preferred when he was home. The meal was served by a short, matronly housekeeper who smiled continually and didn't speak a word of English. She didn't need words, Elizabeth decided, taking an instant liking to the woman. With that smile she could conquer the world.

After the dishes were cleared away and the fire stoked, Elizabeth and Roberto sat together on the sofa sipping grappa which, he explained, was a popular Italian brandy.

She took a tentative sip of the clear liquor and found it very strong but not unpleasant, and it combined agreeably with the fire to warm and ease her weary body.

Under any other circumstances, Elizabeth knew she would have considered the evening a perfect ending to an exhilarating day on the slopes. But with Roberto sitting next to her on the couch, she couldn't relax. Her awareness of him was far too intense to let down her guard, especially now that Maria was no longer bustling in and out of the room. With only the crackling fire to break the silence, she found her tension once again growing.

Watching her he said with a smile, "Sit back, Elizabeth. Relax. Didn't you enjoy dinner?"

"Yes, it was very good," she said, aware that her voice sounded stiff and breathless. "I was just thinking that it's getting late. Perhaps we should be starting back."

"We'll leave soon. When you've finished your drink."

Elizabeth looked down at her glass and decided there was a great deal more liquor there than she'd first realized. Taking a longer sip than was wise, she gasped and made a little face; obviously grappa was not a drink to be rushed. Anxious to keep the conversation going, she suddenly remembered his promise to her in the stable. "I'm still waiting to hear all your dark secrets. From the past."

"I didn't promise to tell you all of them," he said, looking at her over the rim of his glass.

"Come on, that's not fair. I told you mine," she said with forced brightness, trying not to look into those dark eyes or at the strong, classic lines of his face. The Roman warriors must have looked like this, she thought, then forced her mind back to the subject at hand. "Why don't you start with your parents?"

"My parents?"

"You know—mother, father. Most people come into the world with a matched set."

"My parents." He was thoughtful for a moment, then leaned back more comfortably on the sofa. "My father was a quiet man, something of a misfit, actually. He was a scholar by nature and avocation, and unfortunately not in the least suited to breeding horses. But the stables had come to him from his father, just as they had been passed down through so many generations before him, and it was expected that this would be his life." Absently he swirled his grappa, then took a sip. "And to give him credit, he tried his best to make a success of it. But it seemed the more effort he put into the business the more things soured for him. When he died fifteen years ago there was little left except debts."

"So it fell upon you to rebuild Roselli Stables into what they are today." It wasn't a question. His success had struck an Horatio Alger note and had been endlessly pursued by the press. Even today, most articles about Roselli or his horses managed to mention the early, leaner years.

"With me it was different. Unlike my father, I wanted very much to make horse breeding my life."

"And your mother?"

His hesitation was nearly imperceptible, but Elizabeth caught it and wondered if perhaps she shouldn't have asked. "My mother died not long after my father. She never fully recovered from losing him. They were very close."

"I'm sorry. I didn't mean to pry. No, that's not true. I do want to know more about you. But I didn't mean to open old wounds."

"Not wounds really. I don't think about it much anymore. You made me remember how happy they were despite the fact that my father ran a daily race against bankruptcy. I'd forgotten how much they treasured the little things—the picnics they took by the creek in the meadow, their private little jokes, their friends. You know it's funny, but money didn't seem to mean that much to them."

"But it does to you."

"I'd be a liar if I said it didn't. Without money I would have lost the stables, the house, everything my family spent centuries building." He found his mind wandering as the firelight played a lively game with Elizabeth's hair, highlighting the rich chestnut color with vibrant coppers and golds. Resisting the urge to run his fingers through the fiery mass, he thought again how very much he wanted her and how difficult it was going to be to stick to his plan. She had built her protective fences high. If he wanted to break them down he knew it would have to be done slowly, using romance, not pressure. But desire was stinging his body. He hadn't realized being patient could cost him so much.

"But you didn't lose them," she said, prodding him back to the subject. "Your stables are more prosperous than ever."

He sighed, but she didn't catch the double meaning in his words when he said, "Yes, but it is a wise man who does not forget how easily a treasure can slip through his fingers if he does not tread cautiously."

She regarded him thoughtfully as she sipped her grappa. "You don't strike me as the sort of man who's particularly cautious by nature."

"I'm not. But I've learned that there are some things in life worth waiting for."

"Is that why you've never married?" The words slipped out before she could question the wisdom of asking such a personal question. She was surprised to see him giving his answer serious consideration.

"I just haven't been ready to settle down, I guess. At first I was too busy trying to save the stables. And lately—well lately I've had other things on my mind."

Without thinking, he had previously draped his free hand over the back of the couch. Now he thought: another inch or two and I could touch her. He was already bothered by her scent and the way her skin glowed like a delicate peach in the firelight. Restlessly he pulled his arm away and stood to pour more grappa into his glass.

"I see." What she was really seeing, she realized with a start, was the way the muscles in his thighs flowed beneath the tight denim jeans when he bent to put the bottle down. As she stared in fascination, something unsettling stirred inside her and she quickly raised her eyes to find him watching her curiously.

She felt an instant flush of embarrassment and, reaching for her glass, took a quick, sustaining sip. Unfortunately the hot liquor made her catch her breath, and only seemed to increase the peculiar tightness growing deep in her body. When he sat down again, she noticed he increased the distance between them and felt a quick stab of disappointment.

"Maria is always after me on that subject."

"What?"

"Maria—my housekeeper. The woman who served our dinner?"

"Of course. Maria." He was looking at her peculiarly again. Get your act together, Elizabeth, she chastised herself. And your mind off of his arms, lips, and how good it would feel if he'd come over here and hold you. "You say she's after you?"

"To get married. You brought up the subject, remember?"

"Yes, I did, didn't I?" She took another sip of the brandy and decided it had a tendency to grow on you. "I didn't mean to ask such a personal question."

"That's all right," he said, a sexy gleam coming into his eyes. "Since I've met you I don't think you've gotten nearly personal enough."

She cleared her throat and made a show of consulting her watch. "It really is getting late. Don't you think it's time we left?"

"Soon. Don't worry. It's not a long drive."

As he reached forward to put down his glass, he was unable to resist moving closer to her on the couch. She was watching him with those wide, expressive eyes, and her thoughts were childishly easy to read as they tumbled one after the other across her face. He knew she was confused by her feelings, unable to understand the attraction pulling them together. She was too inexperienced to hide her body's instinctive response to his advances. She wanted him yet she was afraid. How very vulnerable she is, he thought. This reminder of her fragility reinforced his determination to proceed slowly.

"Don't be frightened by your feelings, Elizabeth. Listen to them, let them guide you." His voice was soft, reassuring. "Believe me, darling, I would never do anything to hurt you."

Now that he sat closer to her, her mind was spinning again. Part of her was glad he was so near, but with the pleasure came a fresh wave of fear. Why did her emotions have to bounce back and forth like this? she thought in confusion. With Sherman it was so safe, so... predictable. Roberto claimed he didn't want to hurt her, but if she was foolish enough to let matters between them progress any further, he was sure to hurt her whether he intended to or not.

He let his hand settle easily onto her shoulder. When she tensed, he brushed his lips across the top of her hair, whispering, "Darling, relax. It's going to be all right."

Gently he stroked her neck, dipping his long fingers beneath the collar of her sweater to trace the curve of her neck below the nape. "I've been wanting to do this all evening."

"You have?" Her slightly breathless voice touched a bittersweet response in his body. He wondered if she had any idea what she was doing to him.

"Oh, yes." He framed her face with his hands, stirred by the desire he saw in her eyes. He willed himself to take it slow, to remain in control, but his need for her made control perilously difficult. "I've wanted to do this, too."

She trembled as he bent his head, his lips lingering a fraction of an inch above hers, teasing her with their nearness. "Slowly, darling, slowly," he murmured against her mouth, and felt her sharp intake of breath as his hands traveled beneath her sweater to feather over her heated skin. Gently, he ran his fingers up her rib cage to the underside of her breasts, his thumbs lightly massaging them. Through a haze of desire she felt her nipples harden as she waited breathlessly, eagerly, for him to move his hands up just a little bit further.

Sensing her tension, he kissed her below the ear and whispered softly in Italian. She couldn't understand the words, but the rhythm of his musical voice had an hypnotic effect. She closed her eyes and leaned against him as his hands inched slowly upward until they were skimming delicately over the silky sheerness of her bra. When he pulled her forward slightly to unfasten the hook, the breath caught in her throat. She heard him speak, but she was so lost in a sea of strange, wonderful sensations that his voice seemed to be coming from a great distance.

"Raise your arms, *mia d'oro*."

Without questioning she did as he asked, and he carefully drew the sweater over her head and placed it beside him on the sofa. Pulling on the thin straps of her bra, he stripped the lacy garment down her bare arms. The air hit her skin with a little shock, then she was filled with a deep awareness of him as he drew her lovingly into his arms.

Elizabeth tried to understand what was happening to her, but it was like chasing a rainbow; each shimmering, elusive sensation dissolved into another before she could catch hold of it. She wasn't sure what was happening to her, but whatever it was she wanted it to last forever.

"You're so lovely, darling," he whispered, his face in her hair. "So very lovely."

A long, wonderful tremor ran through her body as his hands moved over her back, pressing her to him. "Roberto." She looked into his face and thought she had never seen more beautiful eyes or heard a more beautiful name. "Roberto." She repeated it on a prolonged sigh.

"Yes, little one." He had pulled up her thick veil of curls while his lips skimmed her neck and the delicate hollow between her shoulders. "Soft. Did you know your skin feels so soft? Like the down of a bird."

"I—" With his finger he tilted her chin, raining tiny kisses down her neck and across her collarbone. Then, before she could catch her breath, his mouth dipped even lower to flutter over the gentle swell of her breasts, and a detached part of her marveled at the fact that feelings like this actually existed. His mouth was radiating a fire that seemed to scorch her skin, robbing her of breath, taking away her equilibrium. She felt simultaneously dizzy and crazy and wonderfully alive. She tried to tell herself that she shouldn't be letting this happen, but desire hammered in her ears, drowning out reason. Restlessly, achingly, she moved against him. "Roberto, I—I've never felt like this before."

"I know, darling. I know. It's—all right." His tongue had found an erect nipple and he was teasing it, circling it with the lightest possible caress, gently nibbling it with his teeth.

Elizabeth moaned, her nipples swollen from the tender play of his mouth. He molded her love-sensitive breasts into the palms of his hands and hesitantly at first, then more persuasively, she moved against him, filled with a need to satisfy this strange craving that was firing her body. With a soft groan his lips came back to her mouth, touching, parting, then meeting again in a deep, lingering kiss.

"Elizabeth." The word was a hoarse whisper against her ear. His tongue, his lips, were everywhere, setting fire to each place they touched. Passion flooded her senses, the heat between them building until she felt it constricting her throat, making it difficult for her to breathe. When he undid the snap to her jeans and slipped beneath the fabric to mold his hands to her firm, rounded bottom, she shuddered into shocked awareness. He was taking possession of more than just her body. If she allowed him to make love to her he would be forging a bond she might find impossible to break.

A fierce battle raged inside her between rationality and desire. What was happening to her? Never in her life had she allowed feelings to take precedence over reason. Suddenly she was a little girl again, feeling the pain, remembering the confusion, the broken promises. She thought of the vow she'd made all those years ago and knew she couldn't let it all happen again. Fear rose in her throat and she felt as if she was choking, drowning in emotions she couldn't control.

"No." She pushed at him, taking in deep gulps of air, fighting to put out the fire that was consuming her. "Stop. Please."

Roberto had been aware of her struggle almost before she was. When he felt her hands push between them he immediately loosened the embrace. He knew that she was engaged in an inner battle, but it was several moments before he could bring his own ragged emotions into check. He sat perfectly still, holding her gently in his arms, stroking her shiny, curly veil of hair.

"Shhh, Elizabeth, it's all right," he said. She had buried her face in his chest, and he suspected from the way her shoulders were moving that she was silently crying. Why, he wondered, after so many years of having almost any woman he wanted, was he going to such inordinate lengths to have this one? She was right, he had never been a patient man. Now, for her sake, he had willed himself to wait.

He sighed and shifted her weight a bit so that she rested in the crook of his arm. Reaching for her sweater, he tucked it modestly about her shoulders. Her face was turned away from him, but she was quiet now, no longer crying. Gently, he turned her head until he could see her eyes. They were open very wide and glistened in the firelight from the faint residue of tears.

"I guess it wasn't such a good idea to come here tonight," she said in a little voice. "You should have kept with my original instinct to stay out in the open."

His face softened as he looked down at her, and his voice was more controlled now when he said lightly, "Perhaps we should have dined out in the stable. Diavolo is always delighted to have dinner guests."

She smiled at this, and he felt his heart constrict as he read her unguarded face. Poor Elizabeth, he thought, kissing her lightly on the forehead. Life is not always as it is portrayed in novels.

He reached for her glass. "Here, we will enjoy the fire a bit longer and then start back to Venice."

She took a sip, her eyes never leaving his, then handed back the glass. Her whole body seemed to sigh as she lay back in his arms, allowing the fire and the warmth of his body to envelop her. She felt remarkably relaxed now, finally drained of the tension that had been with her since dinner. Yet even as she closed heavy eyes, Celia's words echoed sleepily through her mind: *There isn't a woman in Venice who wouldn't happily trade places with you.* Now Celia is going to know I'm hopeless, she thought hazily. And I think she may be right.

Roberto watched her for a long time, enjoying the way the flames danced in patterns across her face, thinking about her intrusion into his life. No, he corrected himself, not an intrusion. One didn't call a burst of sunshine an intrusion. Yet certainly she had unsettled him. He had the feeling that after Elizabeth nothing in his life would ever be the same again. In the end, he wondered if it could ever amount to anything more than a fleeting infatuation. There must be a grain of truth in the old adage of opposites attracting, he thought ruefully. Certainly he and Elizabeth were poles apart. Is that why he found her so irresistible?

He sat quietly on the couch holding her in his arms until the fire had burned itself into a deep-red glow. Before he moved he took one last look at her, and for a riveting moment was driven by a powerful urge to arouse her to intimacy while she was still disoriented by sleep. He knew her well enough to realize that it probably would not be difficult. But a quick, easy conquest now, when she was so defenseless, would only serve to drive her further into her shell, make her even more distrustful and wary. A few moments' gratification would not be worth the price. In the end they would both be the losers.

He rose carefully so as not to disturb her, then stretched her out on the overstuffed sofa. From his bedroom he brought blankets which he gently tucked around her, then watched her sigh and burrow contentedly beneath the quilts.

He turned off the one light they had left on by the sofa, secured the grate in front of the dying fire and bent to kiss her lightly on the forehead. She stirred for a moment in her sleep, then was still.

With the amused realization that this was the first time in his adult life that he had left a beautiful woman sleeping on his couch while he spent the night alone in another room, he chuckled to himself and went to bed.

Seven

Strange sounds penetrated Elizabeth's dream. Even as she struggled to hold onto the fantasy, part of her sleeping mind questioned the presence of a horse on a gondola. Roberto was holding her in his arms, caressing her, kissing her, but even he couldn't prevent the boat from tipping as Diavolo pranced back and forth, whinnying and demanding sugar cubes. She cried out but no one came to help them. Then they were sinking, sinking—

She hit the floor with more of a plop than a bang, thanks in part to the thick carpeting and even more to the quilt that had slipped off the couch to cushion her fall. But regardless of the relatively soft landing, finding herself suddenly lying on the floor of a strange room was sufficient to bring her sharply awake.

As the dream faded, Elizabeth made three fairly rapid observations: the sound of horses was coming from the stable, not a gondola; she had spent the night on Roberto's couch; he had not been there with her. Interestingly enough, it was this last bit of information that provoked a rather disturbing internal conflict.

Padding to the window in her stocking feet, she pulled back the heavy draperies to find the stable a beehive of activity. Aside from the horses that were being exercised or otherwise tended, several of them were running around a track behind the buildings. She recognized the lead horse as Diavolo. Then, with quickened pulse, she picked Roberto out of a group of men watching the race from beyond the stable. His back was toward her, but she could see he was following Diavolo's progress through binoculars. He was up early, she thought, then felt a pang of disappointment that he hadn't awakened her to watch the race with him.

Dressing quickly, she followed the smell of fresh coffee to the kitchen where Maria was preparing breakfast. Wearing her ever present smile, the housekeeper led Elizabeth into a cavernous dining room, served the coffee and informed her, through an elaborate system of hand signals, that breakfast would be ready as soon as Roberto came in.

While she sipped her coffee, Elizabeth made her fourth, and most disturbing, observation: Maria hadn't seemed the least bit surprised to find her still there this morning. Was the housekeeper so used to Roberto bringing home strange females for the night that she accepted one more without even batting an eye?

Restlessly, she got up and paced to the door. All right, Elizabeth, she thought, let's get to the bottom of what's really bothering you. It isn't that Roberto didn't bother to wake you up to watch Diavolo work out, or even that Maria wasn't surprised to find you here this morning. What's really eating you is that you slept alone on the couch last night.

She realized this was the height of inconsistency. Hadn't she been the one to pull away during their lovemaking? The word no, if she recalled correctly, had come from her lips, not his. So what in the name of all that made sense was she complaining about?

Irrationally, Elizabeth understood that it was because he hadn't tried harder, that he'd pulled away from her at her first sign of protest as if it was all the same to him whether they made love or not. All right, she thought, feeling she was finally getting somewhere, what you're saying here is that your pride is hurt. Roberto Roselli entertains a female guest without so much as showing her his bedroom, and guest suffers a badly battered ego.

The next logical step, she told herself, was to isolate the reason for such uncharacteristic behavior on the part of the gentleman in question. To this end, Elizabeth pulled out her mental file of magazine and newspaper photos featuring Roberto posed with various women of his acquaintance. To a lady they were gorgeous, sophisticated and glamorous. It was probably safe to say that none of them had ever mistaken Roberto for a gondolier or poured out their insecurities to him atop a bell tower or told off his friends at the opera. She was willing to bet her last reference book that not one of them had been squeamish about going to bed with him because they tended to panic around men.

The incontrovertible fact she decided, humbling though it might be, was that Roberto Roselli had no earthly reason to settle for a nobody little historian, probably a slightly neurotic one at that, when he could have his pick of the most exciting women in Europe. Face it, she told herself, staring morosely into her coffee cup, you and Roselli are not meant to be.

Somehow she had made it through breakfast and the ride back to Venice. If Roberto noticed that her conversation was little more than mechanical, he gave no indication. A few times she noticed him looking at her strangely, but then he'd done that before and she was too upset to care about it now. A couple more hours, she kept telling herself, and this whole crazy vacation would be over. She would politely, or impolitely if necessary, inform Celia that she was leaving early for Scotland and that would be that. No more Roberto Roselli, no more seesawing emotions. The routine of her life would be back to normal. If that sounded terribly dismal, she would just have to learn to live with it.

Their arrival back at the hotel began badly. Before Elizabeth could get in a word of explanation, Celia was fussing over them like two lost lovebirds, and no amount of argument could dissuade her from the idea that they were now an item.

By the time she was finally able to interrupt, Elizabeth was so embarrassed she could hardly meet Roberto's eyes. "Celia, for the last time, nothing happened. I was tired from skiing and fell asleep. That's it!"

"Darling, relax. Your little secret is safe with me." A knowing wink at Roberto. "My lips are sealed."

Elizabeth groaned. "That means by noon half of Venice is going to know I spent the night with Roberto."

"There, see? Of course you did," Celia said, pleased that her niece had decided to be reasonable.

"But I didn't. I mean I was there with him, but we weren't together." She threw up her hands in frustration. "Roberto, you tell her what happened—I mean what didn't happen."

Celia brushed her off with an impatient hand. "No, no, don't bother. Whatever you two are squabbling about will soon pass, trust me." She swept up her coat and shooed them to the door. "Right now we have to hurry. I've made reservations for lunch at Madonna's, then we're off for champagne cocktails and a tango contest at the Cipriani. By dinner you two will have forgotten all about your little disagreement."

Elizabeth's heart sank. The last thing she was in the mood for was champagne and a tango contest. Consequently, when she felt Roberto's hand on her arm as they came out onto St. Mark's Square, she was more than happy to let him sneak her away. She had to admit to being surprised, however, when he led her to an outdoor café and instructed her to sit down, saying, "I think it's time that you and I had a talk."

They ordered coffee and sandwiches and when they'd been served, Roberto pushed aside his food and faced her from across the table. "Now, would you like to tell me what's bothering you, Elizabeth? You've hardly spoken half-a-dozen civil words to me all morning. After last night, I think you owe me an explanation."

"After last night!" Anger rose inside her, then was quickly quelled as she said tightly, "And just what do you mean by that remark?"

"I mean I thought we shared something special yesterday. What did I do to make you angry? I thought I'd behaved like a perfect gentleman."

A perfect gentleman. Her stomach twisted into a knot. Too perfect. She'd rather die than admit to him that she was hurting precisely because he had found that role so easy to perform. She searched for words to get out of this with her pride intact. "It has nothing to do with you. I've got things on my mind."

He was silent for a moment, his gray eyes probing her face as if he were peeling away her pretenses, one layer at a time. His expression was impossible to read; it could have been anything from skepticism to simple curiosity. Too nervous to remain quiet under his perceptive scrutiny, she rattled on, "I've been thinking of leaving tomorrow for Scotland. I have work to finish for Miss Amore."

"I thought you were staying until the end of Carnival."

"I was, or at least it was Celia's idea that I would. This trip was spur of the moment." She laughed nervously, then finished lamely, "You know how she is."

He reached across the table and placed his hand over hers, restraining her restless fingers. Glancing down, she realized she'd been shredding her paper napkin into tiny bits. "Elizabeth, you aren't being honest with me," he said. "Why are you behaving like this?"

It was the same question she had been asking herself for days. Because since I met you I don't know who I am anymore, she thought. Because when you kiss me it's like fireworks and Carnival and Disneyland all rolled into one. Because I'm beginning to like you too much and that could prove very harmful to my emotional well-being. A dozen more reasons flashed through her mind, not a single one that she could share.

Coward that she was, she said simply, "Why go on with something that has no future, Roberto? I'm not interested in a casual affair, and you can't seriously be interested in an historian from Wheat Ridge, Colorado. Last night—" She abruptly stopped herself. There was no sense getting into last night. "With all the Ninas in your life I'm sure you have more than enough to keep you occupied," she amended feebly.

Roberto looked at her for a long moment, then gave her hand a squeeze as he began to slowly comprehend what she meant. So that was it, he thought. How ironic that his high-minded attempts to be noble had so badly backfired. He would have to rethink his strategy. "From that comment I gather that the Ninas in my life do not meet with your approval."

"Since when do you need my approval, Roberto?" Watch out, Elizabeth, he's maneuvering you into treacherous waters. Get back on the offensive. "In case you've forgotten, I'm already seeing someone in the States."

"You mean Sherman the librarian? No, I have not forgotten. But I think perhaps you have over the past few days."

It came as a little shock to Elizabeth that he was right. She'd hardly given Sherman a thought since she'd arrived in Venice. A rush of belated guilt added to her discomposure. "All the more reason to think of him now. It's time I went back to my world, Roberto. I don't fit into yours."

Even as he realized she was voicing the very doubts that had troubled him last night, Roberto found himself strangely reluctant to acknowledge their truth this morning. If anything, her arguments only reinforced his determination to have her regardless of the risks. Skirting the issue he said, "Is that what's bothering you, Elizabeth? The fact that our backgrounds are so dissimilar?"

Elizabeth fought to hold on to her slipping resolve. She pulled her hand away from him and held it curled into a tight little ball in her lap. "That and—other things. I see no sense in going on with this when it can only lead to hurt and frustration." Especially for me, she thought. Because if I let you into my life any further there will be no turning back. "Roberto, please, don't make this any harder than it has to be. Let's just say goodbye and be done with it."

He waited so long to answer her that she thought he was thinking up another argument. Telling herself that being strong now would save having a broken heart later, she watched in bewilderment as he broke into a broad smile. "Actually, you are probably right. In these matters a clean break is always preferable to long, messy farewells."

She continued to stare at him. It was over, just like that. Inexplicably, a huge void opened in her chest. To hide her emotions, she very tidily gathered up the pieces of her shredded napkin and placed them on the plate beside her untouched sandwich. She took a deep breath and stood.

"Well, I guess that's it then. I'd better get back to the hotel and start packing."

He rose, smiling, and helped her with her chair. "I'll walk with you."

Did he have to look so cheerful? "Don't bother. I can find my own way back."

"It's no bother."

Acting untroubled as if they were out for a Sunday stroll, Roberto genially pointed out the history of various buildings as they crossed the piazza, while Elizabeth quietly seethed. If she'd wanted a tour she would have hired a guide, she thought, hurt that he could be so callous. It just went to prove that she'd been right all along. Roberto didn't care one bit about her. She was well out of it.

They reached her hotel. Turning to say a cool goodbye, she was disconcerted when he took her hand and, as on that day in front of the bell tower, raised it to his lips.

"*Addio*, Elizabeth." He lowered her hand but did not release it. "You know I can think of a nicer way to say goodbye. Since you are leaving for Scotland in the morning, why don't I show you one last evening of Carnival tonight?"

She felt the unsteady rise of her pulse as he waited for her response. Having steeled herself for a quick, impersonal farewell, she was disturbed to find herself so tempted to delay the inevitable. "I'm not sure that would be a good idea."

His lips formed a beguiling smile that would have required a far stronger heart than hers to resist. "But it is a lovely idea. After all, it was the way we met. I think it is only fitting that it should be the way we part."

She knew she should refuse, but he was moving his thumb in slow, easy patterns across her palm, and the words she willed herself to speak evaporated before they could be formed. When reason failed, rationalization was more than ready to take over. After all, why shouldn't she go out with

him one more time? After the night before who knew better than she how safe she was in his company?

Because she wanted this last memory of him more desperately than she had wanted anything in her life, she smiled
and said yes.

It was some minutes past eight when they left the hotel.
Hailing a water taxi, Roberto gave an address then settled
beside Elizabeth on the seat. He looked casually elegant in
a light-colored turtleneck sweater and dark-gray wool jacket
and slacks. Elizabeth thought he had never appeared more
handsome and was already having second thoughts about
the wisdom of going out with him. Just sitting next to him
was enough to elevate her blood pressure into the danger
zone. Self-torture, she reminded herself sternly, was not
considered a virtue.

"I can't get used to going everywhere in a boat," she said,
covering her nervousness with small talk. "Where are we
going?"

"To a little bistro not far from the Rialto Bridge. With
luck, it won't be quite as hectic there tonight as other res-
taurants during Carnival." His smile made her feel a little
heady. "Their seafood is famous."

"Seafood is always nice," she said, the words sounding
unbelievably prosaic. Oh, Lord, Elizabeth, must you seem
so dull and proper and—small-town Americana? She decided it was going to be a long, stressful evening.

"How did Celia react to the news that you're going to
Scotland tomorrow?"

"I haven't told her yet." At his upraised eyebrow, she
went on, "No, for once it wasn't cowardice. I haven't had a
chance to speak to her. She didn't come back from Gui-
decca," she said, indicating one of Venice's smaller is-
lands. "One of her friends called and said she'd be spending

the night with them at the Cipriani. I'll wait until she gets back in the morning before I leave."

"Then you haven't changed your mind."

She shook her head, thinking that it wasn't for lack of vacillating. All afternoon she'd fought a battle with her baser instincts. In the end, victory had not been achieved without a price. "No," she said in a hollow tone. "I haven't changed my mind."

Despite Roberto's hopes, the bistro was packed with diners. But subscribing to the adage that there was safety in numbers, Elizabeth was rather glad they would have no chance to be alone in some secluded little corner. As it was, their table was in the center of the restaurant which, as with all public places during Carnival, was filled with revelers whose costumes ran the gamut from the sublime to the ridiculous. One nearby man was entirely covered from head to toe in old socks, while at an adjoining table two couples were laughing over homemade pasta, their faces painted to match their clothes.

"This is the first time in my life I've felt out of place dressed normally," she said, taking a menu.

"Perhaps we should have come as Marie Antoinette and her gondolier."

She peeked at him over the menu. He was smiling at her. "I'd like to forget that entire evening, if you don't mind," she said, lowering her head to ask if *anguille* was animal, vegetable or mineral.

"It's eel," he told her. "And I prefer to remember it as one of the most enchanting evenings of my life."

Another peek. He was still smiling, but close scrutiny seemed to suggest he was sincere. "My memories of it aren't as kind," she said, determined to treat the matter lightly. "I had a terrible headache the next morning."

"And I was consumed by a desire to find the lovely Miss Antoinette who had stolen my heart."

"Now you *are* teasing me."

"Perhaps a little," he admitted, laughing. "But you have only yourself to blame. You're so adorable when you're serious. Your eyes grow large and very blue, and you have a tendency to gnaw on your bottom lip as if you can't decide whether to cry or to run away."

"I do no such thing!"

"Oh, but I'm afraid you do. That's what makes it such fun."

She withdrew again behind her menu. "I'm delighted I've provided you with such good entertainment."

Three fingers appeared at the top of her menu, slowly pulling it down until she was looking directly into those soft gray eyes. Despite her annoyance, his expression touched her with its tender understanding. "You're even more delectable when you're angry. The corners of your mouth crinkle up, and two lovely spots of rose appear on either cheek."

"You're changing the subject. And no, as a matter of fact I wasn't aware I exhibited those particular physiological idiosyncrasies."

"Now I know you're angry. You're beginning to sound like a walking encyclopedia again." She blushed slightly at that. "And I think you're very beautiful, Elizabeth, temper and all."

Her flush deepened and she hastily pulled the menu back up to hide her face. Affecting a sudden absorption in the dinner selections, she again asked his help in translating. In the end, she gave up and left the ordering to him.

They were presented with such a variety of starters she was afraid she wouldn't have room left for the main course. But when the *granseole*, a tasty local crab dish, and the scampi were served, she found a sudden resurgence of her appetite. When she was sure she couldn't eat another bite, the waiter rolled out the pastry cart.

"That's positively sinful," she said, staring at the selections with wide eyes.

"But of course," he said, laughing at her expression. "Elizabeth, this is Carnival. Let down your hair. Eat, drink and be merry."

"For tomorrow we diet." Unable to resist, she selected a flaky, rich-looking pastry covered with fresh fruit and whipped cream. "If I'm going to sin I might just as well do it in style."

When they left the bistro, Elizabeth said she preferred to walk, maintaining she needed some exercise to work off all the rich food. "And I want to soak up all I can of Venice and Carnival before I leave tomorrow."

When he said nothing to dissuade her from leaving, she felt another pang of disappointment, closely followed by a feeling of self-disgust. After all, wasn't a clean break with no looking back what she wanted? It was the only sensible course. The relationship had been a fantasy from the beginning, due to the spell of Carnival, nothing more.

Elizabeth paid little attention to where they were going; the narrow streets and bridges looked much the same to her, especially after dark. It was the fifth night of Carnival, and the city was alive with partygoers—some of the parties happening right out on the street—and she and Roberto played a game to see who could pick out the most outrageous costume.

"Is that what I think it is?" she said, gaping at a man in a lewd and outrageous costume.

Roberto chuckled. "I'm afraid it is. That particular outfit is his specialty. Last year he won first prize in one of the costume parades and was written up in a magazine."

"And they let him get away with it?"

"During Carnival almost anything goes. But things rarely get out of hand. Nowadays, that is." He paused while a group of clowns crossed a bridge ahead of them. "In the seventeenth century, when *Carnevale* was at its peak, the celebration went on for six months of the year. The use of masks became so abused by thieves and lovers and jealous husbands that the Venetian senate finally banned the practice of wearing them altogether."

Elizabeth laughed. "I don't remember that. Just imagine, six months of the year. I wonder how they ever got any work done."

"I'm sure that was the idea," he said, laughing with her.

When they tired of walking, Roberto led her to a nightclub and they danced to a lively group made up to look like the Beatles and laughed at the antics of some of the more outrageously dressed, and inebriated, revelers. As it neared midnight they left the club, and Roberto hired a gondola for a moonlit ride. This time he sat next to her, tucking the blanket around them both.

"Shouldn't you be back there helping?" she suggested with a mischievous grin.

"Never again," he said fervently. "I've learned to hold the gondolier in very high esteem. Poling one of these things is not easy."

"It served you right for leading me on."

He reached out with his arm and pulled her against him. He kissed her gently behind the ear. "This serves me much better," he whispered, his breath warming her cheek.

Sighing, she put her head on his shoulder and marveled at how relaxed she felt. I want this to go on forever, she thought. I never want this moment to end. She closed her eyes and let Venice envelop her in its spell. Tomorrow she would be gone; she would never see Roberto again. But tonight was hers. She would treasure every moment.

The next hour was like a beautiful dream. There was a sense of timelessness as they drifted down the shimmering canals, the moon a full, glowing silver jewel to light their way. The sounds of Carnival seemed distant now, as if even that august festival did not have the power to penetrate their private world of enchantment. The waves gently lapping against the side of the boat lent their own sorcery to her senses, and she felt as if time were moving like the canal, slowly, slowly. Perhaps they *could* go on like this forever.

At some point they passed another group of gondolas, and a rich, lilting baritone sang to them of *amore*. The night was filled with magic and song. Venice had become a romantic fantasy.

"The stars have left the sky to shine in your eyes, *mia bella*."

She'd leaned her head on his shoulder, and his words were whispered so softly against her ear they seemed part of the evening breeze. Raising her head, she looked at him and found herself mesmerized by his lips. They were so soft and moist, the notion of having them pressed deliciously against hers became nearly overpowering.

He lowered his head, blocking out all thought of the moon and the stars and even of the sturdy gondolier who was silently poling behind them. Roberto's mouth descended to hers, with heart-stopping leisure, as if they had the rest of all time to come together. She found herself straining to meet him, her lips tingling in anticipation, her pulse hammering in her throat.

She felt rather than heard her name on his breath as they touched, lightly, warmly at first, then more disturbingly as he gently coaxed apart her lips to deepen the kiss. His lips were firm and persuasive, his tongue moving against her mouth in a way that left her weak and breathless. Her fingers tightened on his arms as she felt herself dissolving into a world where nothing mattered but their need for each other. Not again, she thought, feeling herself drawn into his spell. I can't go through this again and find the strength to walk away. I'm not strong enough. I love him too much.

The words repeated in her numb mind. *I love this man.* It was the last thing she had intended to happen, but it had happened anyway. Her emotions had acted on their own, and her heart had been lost before her mind was even aware of the danger.

"The—the gondolier," she stammered, needing time to digest her staggering discovery. "What will he think?"

"He will think that I'm a very fortunate man," he murmured, nuzzling the curve of her neck. "He would consider me very foolish if I didn't take advantage of this most magical of opportunities." She shivered as he nibbled gently at her ear. "And I assure you I am not a foolish man."

No, but I'm the most foolish of women, she thought, allowing him to resettle her in his arms. The ache of her love was already growing, spreading through her like an all-consuming fire. What am I going to do? she asked herself. How will I ever find the strength to leave him now?

It was very late when they arrived back at her hotel. Their steps, by silent, mutual consent, slowed as they reached the entrance. His hand remained around her waist as she turned to him, and he gazed at her with eyes that seemed to have been touched by the night.

"It's been wonderful, Roberto," she told him, trying to control the slightly tottery quality of her voice. "I'll never forget Venice—or Carnival. Or you." All right, she told herself firmly. Enough. For God's sake, don't get maudlin, and whatever you do, do not invite him upstairs. Celia is spending the night at the Cipriani, remember? To her amazement she heard herself say in someone else's voice, "Would you like to come up for a nightcap?" Was that the correct phrase? she wondered distractedly, dazed that she was actually doing this. Was this the way a sophisticated woman invited a man to her room?

And after that? As the elevator silently ascended, Elizabeth wondered what the sophisticated people of the world did to avoid a broken heart.

Eight

By the time they reached her room, Elizabeth remembered that the only alcoholic beverage she'd seen in their suite was her aunt's sherry. Nervously she combed through her mental archives trying to determine if sherry constituted a proper nightcap, then gave up, deciding there were limits to her sophistication.

"I hope sherry's all right," she said. "It's all we've got."

"It's fine."

Something in his voice caught her attention, and she saw a wry smile on his lips as she fumbled through the cupboard trying to locate the bottle. Who did she think she was kidding? When they handed out sophistication, Roberto had been at the head of the line. He could spot a rank neophyte from a mile away. But it was silly of her to worry. Last night there'd been no Celia around to disturb them and she'd been safe as a baby.

She finally located the sherry, and while she poured amber liquid into two glasses, he wandered to the window to look out at the late-night fireworks that were transforming the sky into a sparkling kaleidoscope. In her nervousness she spilled a few drops of wine and was mopping them up when he turned from the window.

"Would you like some help?"

"No, thank you. I mean how difficult can it be to pour two glasses of wine?" Flustered from his scrutiny, her elbow hit the bottle and she only just caught it before it overturned. Hanging onto it by the neck, she saw laughter twitching at the sides of his mouth. "All right," she said somewhat stiffly. "So maybe there is a bit of a knack to it."

He came over then and put his arm around her, but the amusement remained in his eyes. "I don't mean to make you nervous, Elizabeth. You're doing just fine." He brushed a kiss onto her cheek and walked over to the writing table where he thoughtfully turned his back so she could finish the job without an audience. She watched him pick up the Bentham first edition he'd sent her. Switching on the desk lamp, he carefully thumbed through the pages.

"It looks to be tedious reading," he said.

"There was a tendency to be verbose in those days," she said, relieved to be back on familiar ground. "But parts of it are very interesting."

"Don't tell me you've made your way through it already."

"I studied Bentham's theories on utilitarianism in college. But I reread certain parts to see if I still disagreed with his basic premise."

She handed him a glass of wine, and with a quick, nervous look at the couch, went to sit in an easy chair. His expression as he stood by the desk told her he had not misinterpreted her move. "And do you? Still disagree, I mean?"

"Yes, basically I do. Bentham maintained that the rightness or wrongness of an action is determined by the amount of happiness it produces."

He studied her face as he sipped his sherry. "And what do you think?"

"I think that the end doesn't always justify the means. Humans possess the ability for abstract thought. They shouldn't be governed solely by their emotions."

"I see." He walked behind her and she had to resist the impulse to turn and see what he was doing. Relax, she told herself, forcing down a long sip of wine. You're making too much of this. When he finishes his drink you'll say a civilized goodbye and he'll walk out that door and out of your life. After he's gone you will go to your room and have a good cry. Until then you will remain in control. Even if it kills you!

She jumped six inches off the chair when his hands touched her shoulders. His soft, easy chuckle accompanied the gentle brush of his fingers on her taut back. "Relax, Elizabeth," he said softly. "The nerves in your neck feel like tightly coiled springs."

Not to mention my heart, she thought, closing her eyes against some very mixed emotions. This is not part of the scenario. He is not supposed to touch me like this; it is very definitely not supposed to feel so good.

She wasn't sure when the friendly backrub turned into something less innocent, but she realized that her pulse rate was increasing at a pace roughly proportionate to the forward movement of his fingers. When his hands reached the hollow below her neck and her heartbeat had soared into the danger zone, he abruptly shifted his attention to her upper arms where his fingers ran up and down in long, leisurely patterns.

"Let me understand," he said, parting her hair to either side of her neck so that he had freer access to her shoulders. "According to Bentham what I am doing to you would be considered right action if it produced a pleasant reaction. Is that correct?"

"Mmm," she murmured, her voice low and languid as her body swayed in gentle rhythm with his strong hands.

"I will assume that by that answer you mean yes. Very well, the question now is whether or not my actions are giving you pleasure." He bent his head close to her face. "May I have your assessment, please?"

"They are. Don't stop."

"Now, Elizabeth, pay close attention please. The next part of our experiment gets tricky." His fingers were slowly easing forward again, but she was enjoying the lovely warm sensations spreading through her body too much to care. "Now I must know if you reached this conclusion on the basis of intellectual observation?"

"What?" she muttered, not really paying attention to what he was saying.

"No digressions, please. A simple yes or no answer will do. Have you arrived at the conclusion that I'm giving you pleasure through a reasoning process?"

"No, don't be silly." Guilefully his hands had inched down a bit farther until they were just skimming over the silk blouse above the rise of her breasts. She breathed in sharply and sat very still.

He moved his fingers to either side of her rib cage, barely touching the cool, thin fabric of her blouse, stopping just short of the undersides of her breasts. "Then, by process of elimination," he went on, his voice a husky, sensual caress, "I must assume that it is your emotions that have conveyed this information. Is this a correct assumption?"

"Roberto—I—don't stop, please." His fingers had left her, but the reason was soon apparent when she felt them loosening the buttons on the back of her blouse. Without a word, she stretched out her arms and let the garment slide to the floor. Roberto's gaze moved slowly, caressingly, over the delicate pink lace of her bra and the peaking outline of her nipples as they pressed against the silky fabric in ripening desire. With a satisfied little smile he sat down on the arm of the chair and before she had an inkling of what he intended to do, he had lifted her onto his lap and slid into the chair beneath her. "What are you doing? I don't think we should—"

"Hush, Elizabeth, you're interrupting an important scientific experiment." Before she could offer another objection his mouth had closed over hers, stopping further words. The warm, compelling embrace grew around her, fogging her senses even as she tried to regain some control over herself, over him. His hand found her breast and she was unable to repress a little shiver of excitement.

"I'm still waiting for an answer," he said against her lips. "What do you feel?"

"I feel—wonderful—alive—tingly all over. Oh!" With a single deft movement he undid the clasp of her bra and she watched it flutter down beside her blouse. Her breath caught as he cupped the tip of her breast in his palm, gently kneading her alert, aching flesh until her stomach formed into a tight knot of desire.

"What do you want from me, *mia perla*?" he asked, his voice hoarse with passion. "What do your feelings tell you?"

Her breathing had become shallow when she felt him reach behind her to release the button that fastened her skirt. With a fluid movement that garment, too, made its way to the floor. The tightness in her abdomen suddenly spread lower to touch off a fiery heat when he placed his hand lightly between her thighs, his long, skillful fingers working their feathery, mindless magic.

"Tell me, darling," he repeated huskily. "Tell me what you want me to do."

"I want...oh, I want..." She could feel his hardness beneath her and she was filled with a heady mixture of desire and anticipation. Whatever ability she had left to reason was evaporating like morning dew on a rose. She, who had prided herself on her ability to reason, suddenly found herself adrift in a sea of emotions. So many and confusing feelings enveloped her that she couldn't begin to sort them out. Overriding them all was the need to have him hold her and touch her and put out this awful, beautiful, all-consuming fire he had started. "I want you to love me. Roberto, I want...you."

His voice reached her like a throaty sigh. "Yes, darling, yes. You have me. Oh so soft, you're so...very soft. Oh, *mia amore*, you have me."

With slightly trembling hands he took her fingers and placed them beneath his sweater. Taking a quivering breath, she let her fingers roam, luxuriating in the hard, hair-roughened planes and the smooth flow of muscles. His own breathing became irregular as she explored the tight skin of his lower stomach, and she gloried in the knowledge that she had brought about the soft, love-misted look in his eyes.

"What do *you* want, Roberto?" she asked, needing to hear the words, having to know that he wanted her.

The luster in his eyes burned hot with desire. "I want you, *mia cara*. More than you can possibly imagine. Tonight, I want you tonight."

Then they could wait no longer. With a soft groan he swept her into his arms and rose from the chair, walking across the thick mocha carpet to her bedroom door. "This is what I wanted to do the night I stood beneath your window," he said, laying her gently on the bed. "I thought I would go crazy from wanting you."

Quickly he stripped out of his clothes then joined her on the bed. Elizabeth felt his weight next to her and for a moment was frozen in the realization of what was about to happen. The dream was becoming a reality and she felt a brief surge of fear.

Then his hand came up and ran lightly over her cheek, brushing the curls off her forehead, tracing the graceful curve of her partially open lips with his forefinger. He said nothing for a long moment, just sat next to her, watching the rise and fall of her breasts, understanding the emotions crossing her face. She saw desire in his eyes, and in the soft curve of his lips as he smiled at her.

"It's all right, darling," he whispered, the gentleness in his voice quelling the last of her doubts. "I want to do beautiful things to you. I want you to know what it is like to love, to feel, to share what is in your heart and mine."

Slowly, deliberately, he brought his lips down to hers in a kiss that surprised her with its subtlety. Lightly his tongue circled her lips, then slipped inside to reignite the fire in her veins. Cradling her face in his strong hands, he gradually increased the intensity of the caress until she was arching up to his warm mouth, wanting to feel all she could of his lips.

His hands skimmed over her body, touching the sensitive, love-hungry surface until her skin glowed with desire. She twisted beneath the sweet assault and he brought his mouth back to hers, their tongues meeting in a hot, feverish embrace. All the while his hands massaged and caressed, exciting her to a point of pulsating need.

His lips were sidetracked by the delectable swell of her breasts and he kissed the dark, rosy nipples until he felt her moan beneath him. "What do your feelings tell you now, *mia amore*? Tell me. I need to know."

"I can't, it's too wonderful. All the sensations—it's too hard to think."

"Then don't think, my darling. Just feel, listen to your body, let yourself flow. Just drift with it. I will do the rest. I will take care of everything. I would never hurt you."

His fingers ran down her body, caressing her breast, touching the soft, flat plane of her stomach, fluttering over the curve of her hip to remove the last barrier that came between them. Where the dainty silk had been, his fingers began a slow, persistent rhythm that wrenched at them both, stoking the fires of her arousal until she couldn't breathe.

"Roberto, I—I need you. Please."

Immediately he shifted his weight and, true to his promise, took responsibility for her protection. Then he moved again until he was directly above her. She looked at him through love-glazed eyes, glorying in how strong he was, loving the desire that bathed his face. She had done this to him. He wanted her just as much as she wanted him. Her fingers reached up and clenched his back as he came down to her, feeling and loving the pulsating strength of his shoulders, feeling his warm breath, his powerful thighs next to her legs. *Feeling.* He had accused her of not having any feelings and suddenly she was consumed by them.

"Love me, Roberto," she cried. "Love me now."

With a groan he completed his descent, his eyes glazed with sexual heat as he slowly, gently entered her. "Darling, darling Elizabeth. You feel so very good."

She had no words to answer him, no breath, no thoughts, just the unbelievably sweet ecstasy that was growing inside her with every thrust of his body. Higher and higher he drove them until she thought her body would explode. And then it did, into a million wild and lovely pieces, just like the fireworks blazing outside her window. She cried out as the pinnacle was reached, then watched in wonder as Roberto followed her over the wondrous threshold.

For a long time she wasn't aware of anything but a profound sense of peace. Her body seemed to be floating, languidly drifting, just as it had that evening while sailing on the canal. Roberto held her close, his shoulder against her back. She felt his warm, lean strength and sighed, feeling sleepy and unbelievably content.

When she awoke she found him watching her in the dim light that spilled across the bed from the other room. "You were smiling in your sleep," he said, blowing softly along her hairline.

"Who says I was sleeping?" she said, hardly recognizing the low, contented voice as her own. "Actually, I was reconsidering Bentham's theory."

"And?"

"I've decided he may have a point after all."

"Oh?" he said lazily. "And would you care to expound on your findings, Signorina Bradshaw?"

She felt his warm breath on her ear and snuggled closer. "I'd be delighted to, Signor Roselli. If, as Bentham believed, happiness can be measured by the quantity of pleasure it brings, then tonight you and I set a new record for both the production and the reception of these emotions. That's speaking intellectually, of course."

"Of course." He touched his lips to her shoulder causing her to shiver. "I wouldn't want emotional considerations to cloud your judgment."

"I never allow emotions to cloud my judgment." She ran her toes up and down his leg, enjoying the way his soft hairs tickled her feet. Turning to look at him, she caught a contented smile on his face. "Maybe I should publish my findings. I want to share my happiness with the whole world."

He leaned over and kissed her eyes, and then the tip of her nose. Turning her over onto her back he enjoyed her laughing face. "We might even come out with our own first edition."

"Who knows, maybe two hundred years from now other young lovers will use it as a basis to conduct their own experiments." His hands were sliding gently over her hip, and playfully she threw her arms around his neck and pulled him down to her. "On second thought, I think we should verify our findings a bit more conclusively before we go to press."

"That could take a long time," he said, kissing her lightly.

"I know. Isn't science wonderful?"

Elizabeth awoke the next morning with Roberto's protective arm across her back. She lay very still for a time, savoring the warmth of his body next to hers, listening to the gentle sound of his breathing. Outside, the city was alive with noise and she knew that Carnival was already in full swing. Contentedly she gazed at her travel alarm clock and her eyes flew open to see that it was after ten.

Celia!

He stirred awake to find her sitting up next to him staring raptly at the door. "What's wrong? You're looking at that door as if you expect it to attack you."

"I'd forgotten all about Celia. She could be back at any minute."

"And you're afraid she'll find us here like this." His smiling eyes traveled over her sleep-flushed body and she quickly pulled up the sheet. The smile exploded into laughter and he pulled her back into his arms. "I don't know why you're worrying. If Celia walked in now she'd be so delighted she'd probably serve us breakfast in bed. She's been working on this all week."

Elizabeth made a sound that resembled a low growl. "If you think I'm going to give her the satisfaction of knowing her interference worked you—"

His lips effectively cut off further protests, and slowly they both sank back into the bed. "On the other hand," she murmured, thinking what remarkably talented hands he had, "it's only right to give credit where credit is due." Her voice caught as his lips closed over her peaking nipple. "Actually, some of Celia's ideas are surprisingly good."

Celia still wasn't back when they left the hotel at noon, but by then Elizabeth was floating on a cloud of happiness and didn't care if all of Venice knew about she and Roberto.

He took her to a small outdoor restaurant overlooking St. Mark's, and she thought the eleventh-century basilica looked like a page taken from the Arabian Nights. Then today, she seemed to be seeing everything through a gossamer veil. With a secret smile she wondered if it could have anything to do with being in love.

After lunch, Roberto mysteriously instructed Elizabeth to pack a few of her things, refusing to say anything more than he had a surprise for her. An hour later they were in his car heading north out of Venice.

"I don't remember being on this road the day we went skiing," she said, thinking he might be taking her to his ranch in Feltre.

"We weren't." He gave her a sidelong look and smiled. "Relax. We'll be there in less than half an hour."

The village they entered was like a picture postcard—a charming medieval city of porticoed streets, stone churches and rushing waterways. Elizabeth looked around in enchantment as Roberto parked the car and went around to open her door.

"Welcome to Treviso," he told her, taking a moment to fold her in his arms. "Thirty minutes out of Venice and a universe away." He kissed her lightly on the lips. "I needed time alone with you, *mia gioia*. Without worrying about Celia walking in the door or fireworks going off outside the window."

"I rather enjoyed the ones going off inside the room," she said shyly.

"That kind I approve." He looked around at the peaceful, slumbering town. "Of course we can always set up our own fireworks display here. It might liven up the place."

The happiness she was feeling glistened in her eyes as she looked around the sleepy village. "I don't want to change a thing. It's perfect." Putting her arm around his neck, she lowered his face until she could kiss him. "You're perfect."

"I thought you would never notice."

Sent off with a playful swat to his shoulder, Roberto carried their things inside the hotel. While he checked in, Elizabeth remained in the doorway taking in the quiet, lazy streets, the cool yellow sun sending its long rays through the trees and splattering gold on houses she suspected had been here when Christopher Columbus set sail for the Indies. The air had a briskness to it that reminded her of a crisp winter day in the Rockies. She took a deep satisfying breath and felt better than she had in months. After almost a week of Carnival, Treviso was like a sheltered cove in the midst of a storm.

Their hotel room was small and simply furnished, but to Elizabeth's admittedly prejudiced eye it was utterly charming. They shared a common bath with other guests down the hall, the floor dipped in the middle and the window would stay open only if Roberto propped it up with a wooden coat hanger. She couldn't have been happier if he had chosen a palace.

They had dinner in a *ristorante* which had once been the ground floor of a fifteenth-century villa. Small vases of wild flowers decorated the tables and the wine was served in large carafes. While they were eating a violinist appeared and played *canzone di amore*, a medley of love songs. When he was gone they laughed as they remembered the night Roberto had appeared below her window to serenade her. They ate fresh grapes, chestnuts and apples for dessert. Elizabeth couldn't remember having had a more elegant dinner in her life.

They spent the evening walking through town, exploring the picturesque streets, holding hands as they walked along a bubbling river. Later they watched the moon rise over the Pescheria, a little island on one of Treviso's most exquisite canals. It was a world for lovers, and Elizabeth knew she was collecting memories to last for the rest of her life.

That night they retired to a brass bed with a sagging mattress and creaking springs, with the moon streaming in. They laughed and made jokes about the room and decided they wouldn't trade it for the Ritz.

Still dazed by the Pandora's box of emotions he had opened inside her, Elizabeth had begun tentatively to experiment with them. Even as she made new discoveries about herself, she sought to learn more about him: what made him happy or sad, how she could please him and arouse him the way he excited her. She wanted to experience everything that was available to her and to him—the full, wonderful, mysterious spectrum of emotions.

"I want to make love," she told him quietly, twirling a lock of his hair around her finger, thinking that it felt like cool spun silk against her skin.

He was sitting propped up against the brass head frame wearing only the cotton bottoms to his pajamas. She was curled up next to him, dressed in one of the filmy nightgown confections she had previously looked on with such disdain. Tonight she thought it perfectly suited her mood; she felt loved and pampered and sensuously alive.

"I think that can be arranged." He sat very still, watching her, his eyes dark and full of promise. His voice was dusky and low. "How do you propose to proceed?"

"By one lovely kiss at a time." She nibbled on his ear while she ran her hand across his chest then up to caress his face. "I want to feel everything, do everything, experience it all. Last night you were good to me. Now I—I want to be good to you."

She felt his breath quicken as she leaned down and let her lips brush over his throat, then down his chest to gently tease his nipples. Remembering the things he had done to excite her the night before, she touched him with little kisses, enjoying the clean, slightly spicy smell of his skin, loving the way his soft chest hairs tickled her nose, rejoicing when his nipples hardened and peaked from her attentions. Shyly at first, then emboldened by the desire she saw smoldering in his eyes, she moved lower, tenderly running her fingertips over the taut flesh just above the line of his pajamas.

She felt him shudder slightly and she smiled up at him. At the same time she lowered her hand again and laid it very gently on his warm firmness. This time an even stronger tremor shook his body and he said on a sharp intake of breath, "You learn very quickly, *mia cara*."

"I had a good teacher."

Moving beside him, she brushed the hair back from his face then ran a finger down the length of his cheek, spending some time on the slight cleft in the center of his chin. When he spoke softly in Italian, she pressed her lips against his in a long, deep, endless kiss that made time seem like a gently flowing stream.

He curled his fingers in her hair as she let her hands wander at will over his chest, his stomach, his abdomen. She felt his belly contract, felt the ragged cadence of his breathing beneath her hands and her joy expanded. Love ran through her in pendulous, sensuous waves.

"I love to touch you," she breathed, letting her lips flicker across his firm flesh, delighting in the response she knew she was arousing in him, feeling a heady, wonderful elation that she had the ability to bring him such pleasure. "It feels so good."

"Too good." His voice was a ragged whisper and she sensed he was reaching his limit. "Come here—before I—where did you learn to do that?"

Her smile was full of devilment as she used her tongue to tease the hard flesh around his navel. "I research romance novels, remember? I—'' Her mouth moved lower until she was softly nibbling the waistband of his pajamas. "I haven't worked for Venus Amore all this time for nothing.''

He sucked in his breath as she undid the snap on his pants and let her mouth move below the cotton fabric. "God bless Miss Amore. What you're doing is—enough, darling, enough!'' Desire ran through him, became part of him, demanding, pleading. With eager fingers he removed her nightgown. The sight of her naked, glowing skin nearly drove him over the edge.

No longer able to wait, his strong hands pulled her up until he could reach her lips, his mouth descending in an urgent, hungry kiss. A storm was building inside him. In all his experience he had never felt this way about a woman, never been so stirred by one, needed one this desperately. But because her pleasure meant more to him than his own, he inhaled shakily and gently turned her onto her back.

For a long moment he looked down at her, fighting for control, afraid he might frighten her in his passion. "You are so lovely, *mia amore*. So very lovely. I mustn't—I don't want to hurt you.''

Her smile was so full of love that it twisted his heart. Her voice caressed him, bringing a measure of calm to his jagged senses. "I'm not made of china," she told him softly. "I won't break.'' She shuddered as his hands ran over her fevered body. "Love me, Roberto. I want you to—oh, yes. Please, love me.''

And he did. The emotions she had felt the night before were nothing compared to the driving, sweeping passion she felt as he entered her now. Eagerly her body answered him, moving beneath him, matching his rhythm. Above her, she saw that his eyes were closed, and his face was glazed with a faint sheen of perspiration as he moved inside her. All the feelings of a lifetime seemed to descend upon her at once and she let them lead her. Shuddering, she gripped his shoulders, holding onto him as they soared—blood pounding in her head, wanting him, loving him, following him blindly until he led her shattering over the brink.

Roberto drifted in the afterglow of drained contentment. He watched the moonlight spill through the window and smiled at the sight of the coat hanger. Leaning up on one elbow, he let his finger drift lazily over the soft skin of Elizabeth's arm. He felt surprisingly peaceful, more relaxed than he had for a long time. If only we could stay like this, he thought. But this wasn't the real world. Soon they would have to leave, resume their lives. Then what?

Gently, careful not to wake her, he pulled the covers up over her back, then settled himself against her, enjoying the quiet rise and fall of her breasts against his arm. Tomorrow they would return to Venice, and a few days after that Carnival would be over. Time for her to leave—to go back to her own life. Time also for Diavolo's race. He would be busy then. Busy enough to forget her? he wondered.

Roberto leaned back in the bed and watched the moon outside the window. He lay there for a long time thinking before he finally closed his eyes and went to sleep.

Nine

They drove back to Venice the following afternoon. For the first time since she'd arrived in Italy there were clouds in the sky and a forecast threatening rain by the weekend. That's fine with me, Elizabeth thought, watching Roberto's skillful hands on the wheel. As long as they were together it didn't matter to her if they were stranded in the middle of a monsoon.

Returning to the frenetic pace of Carnival after peaceful, languid Treviso was something of a culture shock for Elizabeth. She would have liked nothing better than to spend a quiet day or two reacclimating, preferably alone with Roberto at his apartment. Unfortunately, they no sooner arrived back in Venice when they were thrust squarely into the thick of Carnival festivities. Ironically, it began that evening with another masquerade ball.

"I'm really not very good at these parties," she told him when he suggested she resurrect the Marie Antoinette costume. "Why don't you go without me, Roberto? Actually I'd prefer to make an early night of it anyway."

"Of course I won't go without you." He looked surprised that she had even suggested such a possibility. "Don't tell me you're planning to withdraw into that shell of yours again, Elizabeth. I thought you'd put all that behind you."

"Just because I don't happen to enjoy costume balls doesn't mean I'm withdrawing into a shell," she told him defensively.

"Then why do you have such an aversion to being with people?"

"I don't, at least not with most people." She stopped, realizing too late how he would interpret her remark. But, unhappily, it was true. Elizabeth didn't think she could stand an entire evening in the company of Nina and the others.

"Meaning that your aversion extends only to my friends," he said, a cool edge to his voice.

She looked down at her hands. "I just don't fit in with some of them. They make me feel so self-conscious, like I've got two left feet."

"You haven't given them much of a chance, have you, Elizabeth? I know you were put off by them the night of the opera, but you were hardly what I'd call congenial yourself." His voice softened, and he took her into his arms. "Believe me, darling, they are not as frivolous as you suppose. Try to judge them with an open mind. I think you will be pleasantly surprised."

In the end, Elizabeth agreed to go to the party. But not as Marie Antoinette. On that point she was firm. After a prolonged, and as usual one-sided discussion with her aunt on the matter, Elizabeth finally consented to go as a 1920s flapper. It worked out better than she expected for other than the fact that the dress was too short—Elizabeth's opinion, not Celia's—and the deep cloche hat a tight fit over her mass of chestnut curls, Elizabeth had to admit the costume was comfortable. Roberto looked pleased, which, she decided resignedly, went a long way toward making the ordeal worthwhile.

And it was an ordeal. Beneath her pasted-on smile Elizabeth fought an uphill battle with herself to be pleasant, not to be argumentative or critical, from the moment they walked through the gilded door. She tried to ignore the seemingly endless stream of beautiful, eager females who kept attaching themselves to Roberto with fawning expressions and gowns cut down to their navels.

Intellectually, she knew she was behaving foolishly. It wasn't as if Roberto were ignoring her; all evening he scarcely left her side. That women seemed to be drawn to him like a magnet was hardly his fault. As far as she could see he did little to encourage them. It was just that darned charisma again. Face it, she told herself, coming to the depressing conclusion that intellectualizing was not lifting her spirits, you're simply not cut out for this sort of thing.

The next morning over breakfast, Elizabeth listened dispiritedly while Celia reviewed the situation between Roberto and her niece. "It's clear the man is extremely fond of you, dear," she began, buttering a crescent roll. How Celia could eat like she did and never put on a pound continued to amaze Elizabeth. "If you play your cards right you should have no difficulty at all in landing him."

"Landing him! Celia, you make it sound like I'm on a fishing trip. Don't you see what an awful mess this is? How can there ever be a future for us?"

Celia paused, fork halfway raised to her mouth, to study her niece. She was startled to see that Elizabeth was actually near tears. The most eligible man in Europe was at her beck and call and the child was crying!

"Elizabeth," she said, putting down the fork. "Heaven knows I've tried to be patient with you, which is not an easy task at the best of times. But this is simply too much. Really, darling, what are you rambling on about? The man is obviously in love with you. And as usual, your feelings are written on your face as plain as day. Why on earth shouldn't it work?''

"Because we're so different," Elizabeth answered miserably. "Last night was a disaster. You were there, you saw what it was like. Women hanging all over him, glaring at me as if I'd committed a capital offense by taking Roberto out of circulation, not missing an opportunity to get in a little dig here and there when they thought they could get away with it. Even the men don't take me seriously. To them I'm just another of Roberto's playthings." She rose and paced restlessly to the window. "It's all I can do to hold my tongue, Celia. And if I have to go to one more party like last night I'm not sure I'll be able to do that."

Her aunt patted her mouth with a napkin, then rose and joined her niece at the window. "I think you're making too much of this, darling. I'll admit the continental scene takes some getting used to, but with time I'm sure you'll feel more comfortable."

She smiled, put her arm around Elizabeth and gave her a little squeeze before she went on fondly, "You love Roberto, darling. No, don't try to deny it. You've never been any good at hiding your feelings. It's obvious he returns your affection—it was clear from the way he looked at you last night. Don't you see, dear, as long as you care for each other all these annoying little problems can be worked out. If something is worth having, it's worth working for. That simple saying helped your late uncle and I more than once during our thirty-seven years together. It can work for you, too."

Celia's words haunted Elizabeth, perhaps because she wanted so desperately to believe them. But her fundamentally realistic nature was already finding flaws in Celia's reasoning. After all she'd been through with her parents, Elizabeth knew she needed to marry a man who would share not only her love, but her hopes and dreams and aspirations as well. All the trying in the world couldn't fit a square peg into a round hole. No matter how sincerely they might want it to work, she just couldn't see how Roberto's lifestyle and her own could ever mesh.

After three more days of dispirited partying, Elizabeth had to admit the truth: it wasn't getting better. The only thing that kept her going were the nights, the long, lovely hours when she and Roberto were alone and nothing existed but their love. But one couldn't live just for the nights, she told herself in a moment of self-honesty. Each dawn brought another new day to get through.

Elizabeth's muddled emotions weren't helped when she received an unexpected call from a very upset Sherman, calling long-distance from Wheat Ridge, Colorado.

"Elizabeth, what is going on with you?" he asked by way of introduction.

Her heart sank. "Hello, Sherman. How are things in Wheat Ridge?"

"Never mind Wheat Ridge, I want to know what's happening to you in Italy. Sally, the library's high school intern, saw your picture in one of those trashy little scandal sheets they sell at the supermarket and has been showing it to the staff. Elizabeth, how did you ever get into one of those awful papers? And who is this Roselli?"

Oh no! Elizabeth remembered the flash cameras going off in her face the night she and Roberto came out of the opera house. Was it possible the story had made its way to Colorado? She felt a quick sting of guilt, realizing it had simply been easier to put Sherman out of her mind than to face up to the unfair way she was treating him. "I more or less met him through Celia," she told him.

"But a tabloid, Elizabeth! What can you be thinking of?"

"I had no idea the story would reach the States, Sherman."

"Then you really are seeing this man?"

Here it was, her opportunity to tell Sherman the truth, to make the break with him if that's what she wanted. The problem was she still didn't know what she wanted. Old habits die hard, and she had known Sherman since high school.

"Elizabeth?" his voice came to her through the receiver. "Are you still there?"

"Yes, Sherman, I'm here." A pause. "Listen, I'm leaving for Scotland in a few days and then I'll be coming home. Why don't we discuss it then, all right?"

"No, it's not all right. Elizabeth, this isn't like you at all. I want to know what's going on between you and this Italian."

"Don't worry about it, Sherman. I promise to tell you everything when I get home."

"But is it serious? Good Lord, Elizabeth, you can't have known the man more than a few days. And think of his reputation! Sally tells me he's an international playboy. I simply can't understand what's gotten into you. You've always been so levelheaded."

"Sherman, I can't explain it over the phone. I'll tell you everything when I get back."

He made a frustrated sound. "Just be sure you've made up your mind which of us it's to be by then," he told her. "Everybody in town is talking about it."

Later that afternoon she and Roberto attended a cocktail party at the magnificent Gritti Palace, then afterward stayed on to dine at the hotel with a group of his friends. But her conversation with Sherman had left her with a dull headache, and she found it impossible to put his accusations out of her mind. He was right; she wasn't the same person who had left Wheat Ridge just over a month ago. She *had* changed. But was it for the better?

Dreading another long, stressful evening, Elizabeth was pleasantly surprised to find herself seated next to an assistant curator from the Archaeological Museum in Florence. Dr. Armani had recently returned from a promising archaeological dig in the mountains north of Verona. When she discovered the excavation might have a bearing on her current research on megalithic monuments, Elizabeth felt her first real surge of excitement in days. She spent the rest of the evening eagerly pumping Dr. Armani with questions.

Later, in Roberto's hotel suite, she could hardly wait to share the news. "They think they've discovered the remains of a prehistoric druid temple."

"I take it that's good?" he said, watching her in affectionate amusement.

"Good! If it's true it would be a major find." She was pacing the floor as she talked, while Roberto sat comfortably in a chair sipping coffee. "It would mean that the ancient order of Celtic priests migrated much farther south than anyone previously suspected."

"I'm delighted to hear it," he said, unable to contain a smile. "But would you consider me rudely inquisitive if I asked what in the world prehistoric druids have to do with you?"

"The megaliths, Roberto. You know, Stonehenge, Avebury? Remember, I told you I was doing an article on megalithic monuments while I gather research material for Miss Amore's novel? Well one of the oldest prevailing theories concerning these monuments attributes them to the druids."

"Oh, yes, the Avebury Stones. I'd forgotten." His smiling eyes wandered over her appreciatively. "This wanton woman I know keeps distracting me from more serious matters."

In her excitement she skipped over and impulsively hugged him. "And she's enjoyed every lovely moment of her wantonness. But Roberto, just think what this could mean to my article. Not only might there be evidence drawing a more definitive link between the druids and the megaliths, but I would be the first historian to trace the order to northern Italy."

"The *Wheat Ridge Globe* will snatch at the chance to publish your findings."

"If I get the story I'm after, the *National Historian* will snatch it up. Wait, I'll get my notes and show you."

She went flying off to the bedroom and those precious notebooks she was seldom without, claiming inspiration frequently hit her at odd hours and she wanted to be prepared. There was something funny and a bit touching about the way she could get so excited about old rocks and ancient civilizations.

If only she could be that enthusiastic toward his friends, Roberto thought. When she was with them she seemed to withdraw into herself, making little visible effort to be sociable. In the beginning, he'd hoped the situation would improve with time, but if anything it was deteriorating. She was like two different women, the one he escorted to parties and the one he held in his arms at night. He found it all enormously frustrating.

Even though this bothered him, Roberto realized that the simple truth was he didn't want to let her go. For the first time in his life he felt the need to be with not just any woman, but *this* woman. It was more than a physical attraction; it was a deeper, more fundamental need, a need he wasn't at all sure he knew how to handle.

He watched her bounce back into the room, notebook in hand, and felt a shaft of desire that nearly sent him reeling. Wonderingly he thought, who would have guessed that after all this time, and all this searching, I would find the sweetness and passion I was seeking in the arms of this naive and difficult American? When am I ever going to get enough of her? When will I be able to let her go?

"Come here, Ms. Historian," he said, once again pushing the troublesome doubts to the back of his mind. "We can go through your notes later. Right now I have a strong compulsion to conduct a little exploration of my own."

Much later, when he lay holding her in his arms, his face buried in the sweet, thick coils of her hair, he said softly, "I have to go to Feltre tomorrow and make the final arrangements for Diavolo's race. The Verona Stakes will be run on Saturday."

He felt her tension, and when she didn't answer he went on, "I want you to come with me. I want you to be there with me when he runs."

Elizabeth's heart sank. In her excitement at Dr. Armani's news she'd forgotten about the race. She knew all Roberto's friends would be there with their glamorous clothes and sophisticated small talk, but she wasn't sure she could survive an entire day of it, especially when it was her only opportunity to see the dig. It wasn't that she didn't want to watch Diavolo run, but the excavation was a chance in a lifetime.

She sighed, feeling torn. "Actually I was planning to visit the dig on Saturday," she said in a small voice. "Dr. Armani has promised to make the arrangements."

"Surely you can go to this dig some other time. The Verona Stakes is run only once a year."

"I know, Roberto. I'll tell you what. Why don't I go to the excavation in the morning and meet you later that afternoon at the track? According to Dr. Armani, the dig isn't far from Verona."

"But it's all mountainous roads." She could hear his annoyance. "And if it's far off the main highway there may not even be transportation. I don't understand why you can't go some other time."

"There won't be another time, Roberto," she told him softly. "They only allow visitors on Saturday. And I'll be leaving for Scotland next week."

He didn't want to be reminded of her departure, and because he still wasn't sure how to deal with it his answer was uncharacteristically gruff. "All the more reason to spend what time we have left together. This race means a great deal to me, Elizabeth."

"And the dig is important to me." She gave a long sigh. "We seem to have reached an impasse."

"Yes, it seems that way, doesn't it?" he agreed sharply.

Sitting up, she switched on the bedside lamp. "Does it really have to be this difficult? After all, I'll be with you when it counts, when Diavolo runs his race." She brushed a strand of hair from his eyes. "And I can poke around to my heart's content in the morning. I think that's a fair compromise, don't you?"

He looked up at her, then ran his finger along the side of her face. "Not really. I would much prefer to have you by my side for the entire day. But if it's the only way you'll agree to come, I suppose we can try."

Roberto saw relief flood her eyes. "Good. I knew we could work it out." She leaned down and kissed him. "Come on, don't look so glum. It'll be fine. I promise."

Roberto insisted on driving her to the excavation site himself early Saturday morning. Dr. Armani had made the arrangements and ascertained that a bus made the trip over the mountains to Verona once each afternoon on the weekend. Today it was scheduled to stop not far from the dig at one o'clock. Plenty of time, Elizabeth assured Roberto, for her to arrive in Verona before Diavolo's race.

She knew he wasn't happy with her decision, and his disapproval became more obvious as they neared the site. Starting with the rain that was predicted for later that afternoon, he went on to worry about the isolated location of the dig.

"What if you miss the bus back to Verona?" he said, eyeing the narrow road doubtfully. "Or what if it doesn't stop? Buses that run this far north are not known for their reliability."

Even as she tried to reassure him, Elizabeth found his fussing rather sweet. "The bus will stop and I won't miss it. Dr. Armani assured me that the laborers at the dig use it every day for transportation to and from town." She grinned at him, her excitement and anticipation growing with each mile. "You have enough on your mind today without being concerned about me. I'll be fine."

She nodded at a small suitcase she had packed with a fresh change of clothing and high-heeled shoes. "Just don't forget to bring these with you to the track, or I'll have to meet you dressed in jeans and tennis shoes. Your friends would love that." She laughed at his expression. "Roberto, will you please stop worrying? Everything's under control. And I promise I'll be there in time for Diavolo's big moment."

Later, she would have cause to rue her promise, but now she was too filled with anticipation to worry about what might go wrong. She had never been to an archaeological dig and a million questions crowded her mind. Her everpresent notebook and a fresh supply of pencils were safely stowed in her shoulder bag, and five minutes after Roberto's reluctant departure, she'd already put his concerns out of her mind.

Dr. Picard, the French archaeologist in charge of the site, was a wiry little man of about fifty, with a hooked nose, brown complexion and sharp blue eyes. His manner, although outspoken and friendly, was precise, intent and he was well-informed as he discussed his findings. And this he was obviously happy to do as long as Elizabeth's patience held out.

According to Dr. Picard, the excavation was yielding evidence to suggest that an ancient religious community had existed here some 4500 years ago. With meticulous care he showed her the artifacts that had been uncovered to date: tools, utensils, artwork, bits of clothing and some seeds of cultural plants, which had proven to be especially revealing.

"Actually, Miss Bradshaw," he said. "Very little is known about the druids. And of course we are still in the early stages of our work here. However, from what I have seen so far, this site may very well turn out to be one of their communities. In the past, that religious order has been associated with ancient Britain, Ireland and France. It would be extremely exciting if we could conclusively place them here in northern Italy."

With the enthusiasm of a schoolboy Picard showed her around the dig, which covered five acres of predominantly mountainous ground and a fifty-foot square radius of fairly level land where they had discovered evidence of an ancient temple. It was here that they were currently concentrating their efforts. Farther on, the archaeologist became quite excited when he pointed out a midden or refuse pile on which he hinged a great deal of expectation.

"It is in the midden, the garbage, if you like," the archaeologist told her in his slightly accented English, "that we find the real essence of a civilization."

He looked so pleased with himself that Elizabeth would not have been surprised to see him rub his hands together with glee. "It is much the same even now," he went on. "We progress scientifically as a culture, but people themselves change very little. Give me a year's worth of someone's garbage," he said with conviction, "and I will give you a psychological and physiological profile of that person. Finding a midden at a dig is like finding hidden treasure."

Black clouds were rolling overhead when Dr. Picard suggested they stop for a bite of lunch before Elizabeth's departure. He refused to listen to her protests that she'd already taken up enough of his time.

"It is always a pleasure to be interrupted by a lovely young lady," he told her with a smile. "Especially one who is both intelligent and genuinely interested in my work."

Over fresh loaves of bread and hot minestrone soup, Dr. Picard gave Elizabeth more specific information concerning the druids for her article. They became so absorbed in the subject that it was after twelve-thirty before she realized she would have to hurry to catch her bus. It had also started to rain.

"You had better wait inside until your ride comes," he said, looking out at the ominously dark sky. "I fear we are in for a real downpour."

When Elizabeth mentioned she was taking the bus to Verona, the little doctor looked alarmed.

"Then I'm afraid you are going to get very wet," he told her. "The stop is half a mile down the road, and there is no place to seek shelter while you wait. That is if the bus comes at all. I'm surprised no one warned you that there is a tendency for the bridge south of the main road to flood in this kind of weather. If it does, the bus will remain on the highway and bypass our stop altogether, especially as it is the weekend."

Elizabeth was beginning to feel alarmed herself. "Is there any other way to get to Verona?"

"There is the train," he said doubtfully. "But that is quite far from here, and the next one will not arrive until four-thirty."

"That's much too late." She pulled up her coat collar. "I'll just have to wait for the bus and hope for the best."

The archaeologist didn't look very optimistic as Elizabeth set off, cursing herself roundly for having neglected to bring rainclothes. Belatedly, she thought of the umbrella in the back of Roberto's car, and the times she had heard him joke that only a fool traveled in Italy at this time of year without one. There was no doubt she'd been a fool, and she had the sinking feeling she was about to pay for her forgetfulness.

There was only a wooden stake painted a faded yellow-orange to mark the bus stop, and as Dr. Picard warned there was no shelter at all. During the walk from the excavation site the icy rain had increased in volume until it became torrential. Ruefully Elizabeth remembered her nonchalant comments about the forecast when they were driving back from Treviso. How easy it was to be brave when you were safe and dry in a car. At this rate she might just get her monsoon, and she would have to face it without Roberto.

By one o'clock she was thoroughly drenched and freezing. By two o'clock she'd given up on the bus and decided that walking was preferable to turning into an icicle by the roadside. Her shoes and pants were soaked and caked with mud, her hair was plastered to her head and her wool coat looked as if she'd worn it to go swimming.

She heard the old truck before she could see it. The brakes squeaked on the slippery road, and the engine was coughing and sputtering so badly Elizabeth was surprised it was running at all. It had a battered cab, a wood-slatted bed in the back carrying some kind of a cow, and one dim headlight. Nonetheless it was the only moving vehicle that had come by in an hour, and she stood in the road and flagged it down for all she was worth. With chattering teeth she watched it stop, or more accurately, skid ten or fifteen feet and slide to the side of the road. To Elizabeth it looked like a chariot from heaven.

There were two occupants in the cab, a middle-aged man and a teenage boy. As she got closer she saw a large, long-haired dog sitting between them. Although the truck's human occupants smiled a toothy greeting, their blank stares soon made it obvious that neither of them spoke a word of English. It was only after several minutes of pantomime that they finally seemed to understand she was going to the Verona racetrack. At least, as the farmer pulled back out into the road, she hoped they understood.

The ride was a nightmare. Out of politeness, or the fact that it was necessary for the boy to hold the passenger door closed with a rope, they had seated her between them. This wasn't too bad until the very smelly sheepdog decided he did not care for the way his seat had been taken and took up residence in her lap. If she thought she'd escaped the rain, a steady overhead drip of icy water soon set that matter straight.

The cab smelled of wet dog, perspiring men and cattle. It bounced about so fiercely it gave her a headache, and on every turn she prayed fervently that the brakes would hold. When they finally reached the racetrack she was so relieved she felt like getting out and kissing the ground. She was soaking wet, muddy, smelly and covered with dog hair, but she was in one piece. For that she was profoundly grateful!

Thanking the farmers in a mixture of broken Italian and sign language, Elizabeth stood for a moment in the rain, which had subsided to a light shower, and tried to decide what to do. She was already late, and considering the way she looked the last thing she wanted was to see Roberto or any of his fashionable friends. But since he had her change of clothing, there didn't seem to be any choice but to go ahead with their plan whether she wanted to or not.

Elizabeth handed Roberto's pass in at the gate, then trying to look as inconspicuous as possible, followed the signs to the owner's section of the stands. Once there, however, she could see no sign of Roberto. Great, she thought, trying to ignore the curious and outright disapproving looks being aimed in her direction. Without Roberto she couldn't get into the enclosed area, and she could hardly continue to stand here as if she'd just come from a mud wrestling contest.

Just then she spied an usher, and waving her arm, managed to catch his attention. Thankfully he spoke at least a smattering of English, and upon being questioned told her that the Stakes race had been delayed because of the storm.

"It will be run soon, *signorina*," the boy told her, looking her up and down disdainfully. "But you cannot watch from here. Owners only."

"Yes, I understand," she said, then hastily scribbled a note. Handing it to him with some coins she went on, "Please give this to Signor Roselli. *Presto, per favore.* Hurry, please."

The few minutes it took for Roberto to appear seemed more like an eternity. Crouching back as far as possible beneath the overhang of the stands, Elizabeth turned her back to the crowd and the rain and pretended to be absorbed in a sign which she thought had something to do with placing bets. Actually she was so cold and miserable she was beginning to wish she'd found some way to get back to Venice instead of coming to the track. How was she ever going to explain her appearance to Roberto, especially after all his dire predictions? And heaven help her if she was spotted by any of his friends!

"Elizabeth?"

At the sound of his voice she whirled around, then stopped when she saw his face. With a sinking heart she realized it confirmed her worst fears. His eyes were very dark, and his lips were drawn into a tight line. "Don't say it, Roberto. I know, I look like a disaster. But I'm here." That had to be worth something. "I kept my promise."

His voice was ominously quiet. "What happened?"

"The bus didn't come because of the storm and I had to ride in a cattle truck." When his expression didn't change, she felt her own temper rising. After all she'd gone through to get here this afternoon, the least he could do was not stand there and glare at her! "If I wasn't so cold I'd make my own way back to Venice. But I—I'm freezing." She was shivering now, holding her arms tightly clasped across her body. "May I please have my clothes?"

Without a word he handed her the suitcase. "You should have been here hours ago."

The race, she thought in disbelief. I nearly kill myself trying to get here and all he can think of is the damn race. "I heard the running of the Stakes was delayed," she said tightly. "I told you I'd be here on time."

For some reason this seemed to make him even angrier, and with an abrupt movement he turned back toward the stands. "You'd better hurry up and change before you catch pneumonia. I'll leave word with the usher that you're my guest."

Elizabeth watched him say something to the young man she had talked to earlier, then as she turned to move away she very nearly collided with Nina who was about to enter the stands with some friends. Elizabeth watched as shocked recognition dawned on the blonde's lovely face. "Miss Bradshaw! Don't tell me that's really you!"

"Roberto's little librarian?" she heard one of the men ask. "What happened to her?"

Elizabeth heard someone laugh and someone else cough uncomfortably before she broke from the group and ran for the nearest ladies' room. Once inside she shut herself into the darkest, most secluded cubicle, resting her head against the cold stone wall. Oh Lord, what next? she thought, no longer able to hold back the tears. You're not very bright sometimes, she told herself.

When she finally had herself back in control, she blew her nose on a wad of toilet paper, then took a depressing inventory of herself. If they were giving awards today for the most bedraggled spectator at the track, she'd be sure to win first prize. Well, Roberto's friends would have plenty to talk about now. She could well imagine what they were saying.

Deciding she couldn't put it off any longer, she removed her coat and sweater and was just coming out to wash up when she heard footsteps. Elizabeth's fingers froze on the door latch when a high, familiar voice said, "Who would have thought she'd have the nerve? I mean, really, coming here today looking like something the cat dragged in."

"It was the smell that nearly did me in," another voice said. "How do you suppose she managed to get in that condition?"

"Roberto said something about an excavation. But he didn't say she was digging it herself."

There was a pause while they laughed. Elizabeth heard the sound of running water and then the second voice said, "Lend me your perfume, will you, Nina? All I can smell is horses, and—" More laughter. "—the little Yankee librarian."

"Did you see Roberto's face? He looked as if he'd like to strangle her. Imagine, embarrassing him like that."

"Even when she's presentable, or perhaps I should say as presentable as she can manage—" Some tittering. "I still don't understand what he sees in her."

"I know. Amazing, isn't it?" A pause while Elizabeth heard the sound of hairspray. "What do you suppose they talk about? I can't imagine they have anything in common."

"Who says they talk?" the second woman said in a suggestive tone.

More laughter. "Don't worry, he'll soon tire of her. She's just been an amusing Carnival diversion. But Carnival is almost over." Elizabeth heard them moving toward the door. "Roberto's smart enough to see she doesn't belong in his world. If nothing else, today's performance ought to open his eyes."

When Elizabeth finally came out of her cubicle the rest room was deserted. Walking to the sink, she splashed cold water on her face, then washed the mud off her legs and ankles as best she could. Moving mechanically, not allowing herself to think, she went back into the partition and changed into a clean dress and stockings, then slipped on the pumps. When she came out again she ran a comb through her tangled curls and stared at herself in the mirror.

"They're right, you know," she told the pale face with the huge blue eyes looking back at her from the glass. "You don't belong in his world. And you know something else, Ms. Bradshaw? I think it's high time you gave some serious thought to getting back to your own."

Ten

___

After the race, the ride back to Venice was silent and strained. Only a little while earlier the air had been charged with Diavolo's thrilling win in the Stakes. Now, Elizabeth thought, watching Roberto's hard, lean profile, they might be on their way to a funeral.

When she could stand the tension no longer, she said, "Diavolo looked wonderful today, despite the wet track."

"He's a good mudder. But then Diavolo runs well on any surface."

More silence.

"When will he race again?" she asked, when the atmosphere again became oppressive.

"Probably in June. I'm taking him to the States."

"I see." She waited, but when it became obvious he had nothing further to add to the conversation she began to grow angry. He'd scarcely said a dozen words to her since she'd rejoined him in the stands before Diavolo's race. "What's this supposed to be, the cold-shoulder treatment because I showed up today looking like something the cat dragged in?"

"Not at all." For the first time since leaving Verona, he looked at her. "But if you really want to talk let's discuss some of the more pertinent issues between us, starting with why you refused to come into the winner's circle with me."

She was momentarily taken aback, knowing he would not appreciate the real reasons she'd remained in the stands following the race. After what she'd overheard in the ladies' room, she wanted to put as much distance as possible between Nina and the rest of the throng who'd crowded into the winner's circle behind Roberto. "It was a madhouse," she said. "I'm not used to so many photographers. Anyway, it was your victory—yours and Diavolo's."

"And one you didn't care to share with me?"

"That's not it, Roberto. I just—I just didn't feel as if I belonged out there." She remembered the women who'd been more than happy to share the limelight with him. "Besides, you didn't exactly look lonely out there. As I recall you had your arms amply full while they were snapping pictures."

"If you mean Nina and Danielle, they were just window dressing. It's good publicity for the track and expected by the press." He gave her another sidelong look. "It could have been you."

"Yes, I suppose it could have been," she agreed quietly, wanting to change the subject. It was no longer her concern how many beautiful women fell into his arms, whatever the reason. "But I think I caused enough commotion for one day without providing more grist for the gossip columnists."

"The tabloids will pounce on anything. You have to ignore them."

"I'm afraid that's a talent I may never cultivate. I can't get used to seeing my name in the society section. Stories about us have even reached Wheat Ridge."

He glanced at her. "Sherman?"

She nodded. "He called a couple of days ago. He was understandably upset."

"And you confirmed the fact that you'd been seeing me?"

"Mainly I evaded him, and the truth. He said I'd changed." She looked at Roberto. "He's right, you know. For the last week I've been living a kind of fairy tale."

"Is that so bad, Elizabeth? Most people would give a great deal to live out their dreams."

"Dreams are nice while they last, Roberto," she said quietly. "But inevitably the time comes when you have to wake up and face the real world again."

His voice had become very low. "What else did you tell Sherman?"

"That I'd be leaving in a few days for Scotland, and that after that . . . I'd be coming home."

He was quiet for a moment. "Then you've made up your mind."

No, I haven't made up my mind, she thought, amazed that it could hurt so much to say goodbye. It's been made for me—what choice do I have? Suddenly the days ahead loomed bleak and meaningless. They say time heals all wounds, she told herself. Dear God, I hope that's true. "I should have left days ago, Roberto. We both know that."

Stopping the car at a signal, he gave her a long look. "Do we, Elizabeth? Perhaps we wouldn't if you weren't so stubborn."

She looked at him sharply. "Stubborn? Just what do you mean by that?"

"For one thing, you didn't really have to go to the excavation today. I'm certain I could have arranged a private visit with this Dr. Picard and set it for a more convenient time. Dammit, Elizabeth, you knew how important this race was to me, yet you deliberately did your best to avoid going.''

"Are you suggesting that I personally arranged the storm, Roberto? How very clever of me.''

The signal changed and he shifted angrily into traffic. "If you'll recall I warned you about the weather front *and* the possibility of the bus not getting through. You chose to go anyway.''

She clamped her lips shut to keep from shouting at him. "Visiting the dig meant a great deal to me. I had no idea the storm would be so severe.''

"Come on, Elizabeth, admit the truth. The real reason you were so adamant about going to that infernal dig today was because you're uncomfortable around my friends.''

"Yes, I'm uncomfortable. They go out of their way to make sure I feel that way. To them I'm nothing more than an amusing little hick librarian they can look down their long, patrician noses at.''

"And what have you done to win them over?'' he asked hotly. "You don't make the slightest attempt to cultivate their friendship.''

"Cultivate their friendship? Roberto, people like that don't have friends, they have acquisitions. They surround themselves with acquaintances who either make them look good or add to their financial status. I don't do either so they make jokes about me behind my back.''

"You in turn either insult them with that sharp tongue of yours or avoid them altogether. And today you top it off by showing up at the Stakes two hours late and—''

"Looking like a half-drowned rat?'' she offered bitterly. "No, don't say anything else. I get the point. I've humiliated you in front of your friends. Well I think you'll understand when I say it was a bit embarrassing for me, too.''

She stared stonily ahead, willing herself not to break down in front of him. "I think we've just about covered all the pertinent points, Signor Roselli. Now, if you will kindly take me back to my hotel I'll say *arrivederci* and remove this embarrassment from your life."

"Fine," he answered, taking a turn too sharply. "Why don't I do just that."

For as long as it took her to go upstairs in the elevator, Elizabeth nurtured a faint hope that she might somehow keep the day's events from Celia. Of course, the idea was foolishness itself. Celia's private grapevine had already reported in with all the juicy details. Rarely had Elizabeth seen her aunt in such a state of nervous agitation. She was pacing the room while fortifying herself with a bottle of Soave Bianco ordered from room service.

"I almost died of mortification when I heard the news." She took a long, bracing sip of her wine. "Darling, really! However did you manage to get yourself in that—odoriferous condition?"

In a few terse words, Elizabeth outlined the more salient parts of her day, concluding with a considerably capsulized version of her fight with Roberto during the ride back to Venice. "I'll be leaving for Scotland in the morning," she ended in flat tones. "I should have left days ago."

"You'll do no such thing," her aunt said emphatically. "Obviously you and Roberto have had words over this, which I must say is completely understandable. If you leave now without resolving your differences, you'll have the rest of your life to regret it."

"The only thing I regret is that I ever came to Venice in the first place, Celia."

"You say that now, but when you've had time to cool down you'll feel differently." She finished her wine, poured another glass and resumed pacing. "The thing we must resolve, of course, is how to get Roberto to come around without letting him know that you care. It never does to encourage a man when he's feeling sorry for himself. Makes him insufferable to live with later.''

"Believe me, Celia, I honestly don't care if Roberto comes around or not. And since I'll never have the privilege of living with him, he can feel sorry for himself until he's blue in the face. This whole thing has been a mistake from the beginning, a mistake I intend to rectify as soon as possible.''

Celia ceased her pacing to give her niece a long, hard look. "Darling, sometimes I truly wonder why I bother. All right, all right,'' she went on with a long sigh, "I can see that you've made up your mind to leave. But at least wait one more day, if for no other reason than to see the last night of Carnival. Believe me, dear, it's a sight you don't want to miss. And what possible difference can it make in your plans? The snow will still be waiting for you in Inverary, and you can slosh about to your heart's content.''

In the end Celia won, although Elizabeth didn't try to deny that this time it was because she wanted her to. Rational thought to the contrary, she couldn't help nursing a secret hope that Roberto would call, that they might still patch things up, that it didn't have to end like this. But by Monday morning, even Celia couldn't convince her that there was any further reason to delay her departure.

"He knew where to call,'' she told her aunt, discarding the last flimsy shred of pretext. "Obviously, he had nothing more to say to me.'' She had finished packing. As an afterthought, she placed Bentham's book in her suitcase before closing it. "Face it, Celia, it's over. It's time I got on with my life.''

What difference did it make how it ended? she asked herself as she sat on the bus that would take her to Venice's Marco Polo airport. Inevitably it would have come down to this even without the scene at the racetrack. She had to get back to the real world sooner or later. When you play with fire, she thought derisively, you'd better not complain if you get burnt. But until you've really loved you just don't know how much it's going to hurt.

Fittingly perhaps, the unusually fair weather had given way to a freezing rain the night before, and as the bus started for the airport, she looked back on a picture postcard scene: snow-topped roofs set off by thin ribbons of blue-green canals. The last sound she heard was the bells of San Marco ringing out the end of Carnival and the beginning of Lent. Tears stung her eyes as she realized they were also ringing the end to the most exciting ten days she had ever known. She knew that after Roberto nothing in her life would be quite the same again. And, she realized sadly, neither would she.

As Celia predicted, Scotland was very cold. After flying into Glasgow airport, Elizabeth rented a car and made the picturesque drive north along Loch Lomond, then west around the head of Loch Fyne to Inverary.

Normally the tiny village, which was a classic example of eighteenth-century Scottish town planning, would have captivated her. It was so rich in ancient and medieval monuments and castles that she could have spent days sloshing about, as Celia called it. But despite its beauty and rich heritage, Elizabeth found it difficult to be properly appreciative. After the frenzy of Carnival, rural Scotland seemed anticlimactic—incredibly remote and lonely.

For a week she trudged around the village and the neighboring countryside, armed with notebook and camera and profound rancor toward Tennyson for suggesting that loving and losing were preferable to not having loved at all. Obviously the man had never personally undergone the experience or he would never have written such nonsense.

During this time there were several light snowstorms, but nothing that came even close to Celia's visions of deprivation in the outer regions of civilization.

Eventually her research led her north toward Cladich, as she followed the path Miss Amore's hero would take to raise Highland regiments in support of the Hanoverians. In Cladich, by Loch Awe, he would singlehandedly fight his way through the villain's armed garrison to rescue the beautiful heroine from her dastardly captor. His mission successfully completed, he would bolt onto his trusty steed and gallop with her back to his castle in Inverary.

Then carry her to his bed, Elizabeth thought despondently, remembering that Miss Amore's characters had a tendency to end their adventures in a horizontal position. She couldn't remember a single Amore epic that hadn't provided the reader with a happy ending. "Get real, Venus," she muttered, finding she had lost her enchantment for happy endings. "Love stories don't always end happily, or in bed!"

Celia's predicted storm hit the day before Elizabeth's planned departure to Inverary. It was the stuff of nightmares: temperatures that dipped alarmingly below the zero mark, gale-force winds, no power, electricity or phones, and of course, all roads impassable.

Elizabeth's first consolation was that she was stranded in an inn that seemed to possess an endless supply of candles, at least one fireplace in every room and a large gas range. As Mrs. Campbell optimistically put it, "We can all remain snug as bugs until Easter."

Glynis and John Campbell provided Elizabeth with her second reason to be thankful. Although she hoped to be out of Cladich long before Easter, she couldn't think of a nicer couple with whom to share her isolation. Glynis was in her fifties, short and a bit plump with blond hair turning to gray, laughing hazel eyes and a friendly, loquacious personality. Elizabeth was amazed the woman remained so energetic after having brought five children into the world, coupled with working nearly thirty years as maid, cook, bookkeeper and general manager of the Campbell's six-bed inn.

Glynis's husband John was at least six feet two, with pale-blue eyes, reddish-gray hair, a ruddy complexion and a tendency to speak only when absolutely necessary, and then through penurious use of short grunts and little shrugs. Elizabeth thought the two were the most incongruous couple she had ever seen. They were also, after thirty-two years of marriage, still very much in love.

Elizabeth spent the first two days of the storm polishing her research notes. Then, since there was no way to submit them to Miss Amore short of mental telepathy, she suddenly found herself with a good deal of free time. She could no longer avoid thinking about Roberto and deciding how their brief but traumatic interlude was going to affect the remainder of her life.

The first change it had made, of course, was in her feelings for Sherman. There was no longer any question in Elizabeth's mind that there was no future for them. Her mind went back to that rainy afternoon in the Lacock tearoom when her life had been so comfortable and safe, planned out to the last tedious detail. How could everything turn upside down in such a short time? she wondered. Poor Sherman, she would miss him. But better that than a lifetime of mediocrity.

The storm ended abruptly on the third day, after dumping six feet of snow on the countryside. But with a twinkle in her eye, Mrs. Campbell assured Elizabeth that it would very likely be some days before the small arteries leading off the main road would be cleared.

"Donald MacKirdy's in charge of snow removal, lass," the woman informed her. "And he insists on doing the removing according to priorities. The main road running from Inverary to Cladich will be cleared first, then the ones that lead to the hospital, the schools and the churches. Since there are only a few scattered farms past our inn, he'll likely leave our road until last.''

Five days after the onset of the storm Elizabeth was still at the Campbell's inn and beginning to wonder if she might be spending Easter there after all. The phone and power lines continued to be out—evidently they weren't considered priority items, either—and snowdrifts still clung halfway up the ground-story windows.

But if the Campbells were disturbed by these circumstances, Elizabeth couldn't detect it from their actions. Glynis still hummed contentedly as she went about her work, and John's grunts and shrugs were as unperturbed as ever. In fact, one evening after dinner she came downstairs unexpectedly to find the two curled together in front of the fire like a couple of newlyweds, seemingly oblivious to the fact that they were snowed in, miles from town, and with no help in sight.

The next morning, Elizabeth asked Mrs. Campbell about this while she helped her clean up after breakfast.

"Bless you, there's no mystery," the woman told her, laughing. "The very fact that we're so different has actually helped us stay together all these years." She winked at Elizabeth. "It adds a bit of spice to a marriage, if you know what I mean."

"I'm not sure that I do, Mrs. Campbell," Elizabeth admitted. "I've heard that opposites attract, but isn't it important to share things in common?"

"You'd be surprised at what we share, lass." Her hazel eyes softened as she went on. "John may not chatter away all day like I do, and I may not care much for soccer games on the telly, but we both love a beautiful sunset, or fishing for trout on the loch, or just taking an early morning walk through the meadow while the dew is still on the wild-flowers. Nothing fancy, mind, but when all's said that's the kind of sharing that counts."

"I'm sure it's helped that you both have similar back-grounds, too," Elizabeth said, touched by the misty look in the older woman's eyes.

"Similar? Oh, my, lass, that's a good one. I was born and raised in Edinburgh—my mum was a schoolteacher and my dad a dentist. I was going to be a teacher, too, and my degree from the university was in education. Then one day I went with my friends on a church outing to Inverary and met John. His dad was caretaker at the castle, you see, and when I saw this great big, strapping fellow with bright-red hair and bashful blue eyes, I fell in love on the spot. It took John more than a year to get up the nerve to ask Dad for my hand. What a ruckus that brought on, I can tell you." She laughed and again her eyes misted at the memory. "In the end though, it worked out. John still doesn't say more than half-a-dozen words to my parents, but you should see he and Dad during a soccer game!"

Mrs. Campbell went to the stove and poured fresh coffee into their cups. As she did, Elizabeth thought of Sherman and the terrible mistake she had so narrowly averted. At least one good thing had come out of Carnival, she thought, envying the Campbell's happiness.

"In the end a relationship is what you make of it," Mrs. Campbell said, sitting down at the table. "If you put in the effort and a good bit of love, it'll work, never mind the differences. Bless you, darling, if you're lucky enough to find a man who sets your heart to jumping, for heaven's sake don't let him get away!"

Elizabeth had taken to snowshoeing out to the road every morning to see if it had been cleared yet. The weather had been clear for days, but the drifts were still several feet thick.

There was no way she was going to get her car through until Donald MacKirdy decided to put their road on his list of priorities. Not for the first time she remembered Celia's dire predictions about Scotland in February, and thought that in some ways it was depressing to have an aunt who was nearly always right. Unfortunately, she hadn't been right about Roberto.

It had been three weeks now since she'd seen him. What was he doing? she wondered. Did he miss her, or was he too busy to care that she was gone? She thought ruefully about Mrs. Campbell's advice. Sometimes finding a man that set your heart jumping only led to frustration and hurt.

On the sixth day Elizabeth tied on the snowshoes as usual and plodded out to the road. Before she reached her usual lookout hill, however, she noticed a spray of snow flying up in the distance. Hastening her steps up the gentle mound she spotted a snowblower about a hundred yards away. It seemed as if their insignificant country road had finally found a place on Mr. MacKirdy's list.

Elizabeth waved as he got closer, then stopped, arm still raised, the other shading her eyes against the glare of sun reflecting blindingly off the snow. Somehow the dark-haired man driving the heavy machinery didn't look like a Donald MacKirdy. He looked much more like—

Roberto!

Roberto saw shock freeze her face as he brought the snowblower to a stop and killed the engine. In one fluid movement he propelled himself out of the cab and onto the snow, then with quick, purposeful steps made his way through the deep drifts. He stopped when he reached the foot of the little mound where she was standing.

She continued to stare at him, trying to comprehend that he wasn't some wild figment of her imagination. He certainly seemed real enough, standing there in his heavy parka and snow boots, his dark eyes every bit as probing as her own. But why? How? It was just too crazy to assimilate.

"Roberto? What in the world are you doing here?"

"I came looking for you, of course." His voice was edged with concern as he stood not making another move toward her, just looking. "Although you seem remarkably fit for a woman dying of exposure."

"Dying of exposure?" She looked honestly bewildered. "Where did you get that idea?"

"The hotel in Inverary told me you'd taken off a week ago to follow some roundabout road to Cladich. The manager said you expected to be back in a couple of days."

"I did, but the storm—"

"Exactly, the storm," he said shortly. "For three days I sat in the damn hotel imagining you buried beneath some snowdrift, caught in the storm while you were poking about for bits and pieces of old rocks. As soon as it was possible to get through on the main road I drove up as far as the hotel in Cladich where they said you'd taken off northeast looking for some castle or other."

"The Black Duke's castle, where he hides the heroine in Miss Amore's latest—"

Roberto held up a hand. "No, please, don't tell me. I don't want to hear another word about Miss Amore's latest bodice-buster. You don't know how I've been cursing that woman this past week, dragging you off to Scotland at this time of year—"

"Oh, no. Now *you* stop. You sound just like Celia." Her voice softened. "But why did you think I might be in trouble?"

"Oh, no reason in particular," he said, spreading his arms in frustration. "Except that you tend to take evening rides on Venetian canals without so much as a sweater, and you seem to enjoy trudging through mud and riding in cattle trucks during rainstorms and worrying people half out of their minds by arriving two hours late. If anyone could get herself into trouble in all this muck it would surely be you."

She looked at him wonderingly. "You were really worried about me? That day at the track?"

"I was very close to calling out the *polizia*. Why did you think I was so upset when you arrived?"

"I thought you were angry at me for being such a mess."

He shook his head. "Oh, Elizabeth. Beautiful, sensible, foolish Elizabeth. Sometimes I think you don't know me very well. I was angry when I saw you because I knew how easily you might have been injured up in those mountains during the storm."

"And your friends?"

He made a dismissive gesture. "They buzzed about you for a time, then someone else took their fancy. But I soon discovered I could not put you out of my mind so easily. Finally, it only seemed sensible to come here and tell you so. Then when this idiot in Cladich refused to put the northeast road on his ridiculous list of priorities I rented the plow and took off for this—Black Duke's castle."

She stared at him, astonished, her mind whirling with the crazy image of Venus Amore's Scottish hero charging across the countryside to save his lady love. "You *rented* this? Just to look for me?"

"It was either that or come after you on cross-country skis. I thought the snowblower was a good deal more practical."

"But why did you come to Scotland, Roberto?" The pulse in her throat was beating so erratically she barely recognized her own voice. "Why did you come to Inverary in the first place?"

He moved then, taking a step or two closer before he stopped. He was looking at her with that strange intensity that made her feel he could see right into her soul. Elizabeth fought the urge to rush into his arms, to feel his warmth around her again, never mind that it would open the wound that had only just begun to heal. She was holding her breath, waiting for him to answer. I can't take it, she thought, the blood pounding in her head. "Why?" she repeated, her voice a raw whisper.

"Because I love you, *mia d'oro*. Because when you left I realized how terribly empty my life had become. The things I considered important suddenly didn't matter anymore. Without you—"

"Wait a minute," she said, interrupting him, intent only on making sure she had not misunderstood. "Would you go back to the beginning—to the I love you part?"

His eyes softened, and she thought they had never looked so beautiful. "I love you, Elizabeth. If you'll permit me, I will probably say those words until you are thoroughly tired of hearing them." He started to move closer then, but she had already crossed the distance between them and thrown herself into his arms.

"Never," she breathed against his chest. "Those are three words I will never get tired of hearing. But when did you change your mind? I thought I'd never see you again. Even now, I'm not sure your coming here wasn't a mistake."

"No, darling, it's no mistake. Believe me. When you first left I, too, thought it was for the best. Like you I had convinced myself that our love was hopeless. Then as the days passed I realized my life had changed since I'd met you—nothing was the same. I tried to lose myself in the usual round of parties, but I found they only made the loneliness more intense."

He was gazing down at her as if he could hardly believe she was in his arms. He raised his gloved hands to her face and she closed her eyes as the soft cashmere molded her cheeks, as his fingers brushed tears of happiness from her eyes.

"In the beginning, rebuilding the stables was a challenge, every day was an exciting adventure. But as I began to achieve my goals I gradually lost touch with the things that really mattered in my life." He ran his finger, feather-soft over the line of her cheek. "You were the best thing to happen to me in a long, long time. I was bored, dissatisfied with my life without understanding why. But you were real, down-to-earth, loving the funny little bits and pieces of life that had nothing at all to do with money and position. You brought the important things back to me, *mia gioia*. But I was too blind to see."

"But your friends—Roberto I'm never going to fit in with them."

"Shhh, darling," he said, kissing her softly on the lips. "I don't want you to. I have been very, very foolish. This past week I have asked myself so many times if you would ever be able to forgive me."

"I love you, Roberto." She closed her eyes and pressed her face against his chest. "There's nothing to forgive."

He lifted her chin with his gloved finger, then lowered her head to give her a lingering kiss. "I want you to marry me, *mia bella*. I want you to come back to Italy and be my wife. I need you, darling. I cannot imagine my life without you."

And she needed him. With all her heart she wanted to say yes, but the part of her that remained a realist wouldn't let her agree until they had examined every possible obstacle. "Our backgrounds, our cultures, Roberto. They're so different."

"That is what I'm counting on, darling," he whispered. Then, unknowingly echoing Mrs. Campbell's words he added, "We'll use those differences, Elizabeth. We'll use them to keep our marriage fresh and exciting."

Elizabeth smiled and thought about the sprightly innkeeper. She had certainly found a man who could make her heart jump, and she would surely spend the rest of her life regretting it if she allowed him to get away. "It's a risk," she told him, looking into the eyes that could make her heart melt even when it was surrounded by miles of snow. "But an expert I know happens to share your views on the subject."

"I love you so much," he breathed, burying his lips in her hair. "And you can't believe how much I want you. Three weeks can be an eternity."

She felt the longing in his body as he pressed her closer and smiled at the thoughtfulness that prompted him to reassure her there'd been no one else during the time they'd been apart. I love this man more than life itself, she thought, and wondered at the intensity of her feelings. Feelings! Wonderful, glorious feelings!

"It's been too long," she agreed, reaching for his lips. "Much, much too long."

Then they were deluging each other in a rain of kisses. Laughing, they pulled apart while Roberto looked around at all the snow. There was a wicked gleam in his eyes as he suggested, "I've never made love in a snowbank before, but I'm game if you are."

"I've waited too long for this to risk your getting frostbite on a rather important—" a discreet ahem "—personal part of your anatomy." She laughed at his expression and took him by the hand. "It just so happens that I have a perfect room complete with a fireplace back at the inn. Much cozier for what I have in mind. You can park your plow here and let MacKirdy deal with it, if and when he ever decides to put us on his priority list."

"Signorina Bradshaw," he said, feigning shock. "Are you making improper suggestions to me?"

She reached up on tiptoe and kissed him. "Terribly improper. Am I frightening you away?"

He pulled her into his arms and deepened the kiss until she was almost ready to take him up on his offer to make love in the snow. "You could never do that. I love you, *mia amore*," he whispered against her ear. "And you are stuck with that for the rest of our lives."

"That suits me just fine, *signore*." He heard the joy in her voice and thought that, before now, he had never really known what true happiness was all about.

"If this is Carnival Madness," she went on softly, "then I never want to be sane again."

* * * * *

*... and now an exciting short story
from Silhouette Books.*

*

HEATHER GRAHAM POZZESSERE
Shadows on the Nile

CHAPTER ONE

Alex could tell that the woman was very nervous. Her fingers were wound tightly about the arm rests, and she had been staring straight ahead since the flight began. Who was she? Why was she flying alone? Why to Egypt? She was a small woman, fine-boned, with classical features and porcelain skin. Her hair was golden blond, and she had blue-gray eyes that were slightly tilted at the corners, giving her a sensual and exotic appeal.

And she smelled divine. He had been sitting there, glancing through the flight magazine, and her scent had reached him, filling him like something rushing through his bloodstream, and before he had looked at her he had known that she would be beautiful.

John was frowning at him. His gaze clearly said that this was not the time for Alex to become interested in a woman. Alex lowered his head, grinning. Nuts to John. He was the one who had made the reservations so late that there was already another passenger between them in their row. Alex couldn't have remained silent anyway; he was certain that he could ease the flight for her. Besides, he had to know her name, had to see if her eyes would turn silver when she smiled. Even though he should, he couldn't ignore her.

"Alex," John said warningly.

Maybe John was wrong, Alex thought. Maybe this was precisely the right time for him to get involved. A woman would be the perfect shield, in case anyone was interested in his business in Cairo.

The two men should have been sitting next to each other, Jillian decided. She didn't know why she had wound up sandwiched between the two of them, but she couldn't do a thing about it. Frankly, she was far too nervous to do much of anything.

"It's really not so bad," a voice said sympathetically. It came from her right. It was the younger of the two men, the one next to the window. "How about a drink? That might help."

Jillian took a deep, steadying breath, then managed to answer. "Yes . . . please. Thank you."

His fingers curled over hers. Long, very strong fingers, nicely tanned. She had noticed him when she had taken her seat—he was difficult not to notice. There was an arresting quality about him. He had a certain look: high-powered, confident, self-reliant. He was medium tall and medium built, with shoulders that nicely filled out his suit jacket, dark brown eyes, and sandy hair that seemed to defy any effort at combing it. And he had a wonderful voice, deep and compelling. It broke through her fear and actually soothed her. Or perhaps it was the warmth of his hand over hers that did it.

"Your first trip to Egypt?" he asked. She managed a brief nod, but was saved from having to comment when the stewardess came by. Her companion ordered her a white wine, then began to converse with her quite normally, as if unaware that her fear of flying had nearly rendered her speechless. He asked her what she did for a living, and she heard herself tell him that she was a music teacher at a junior college. He responded easily to everything she said, his voice warm and concerned each time he asked another question. She didn't think; she simply answered him, because flying had become easier the moment he touched her. She even told him that she was a widow, that her husband had been killed in a car accident four years ago, and that she was here now to fulfill a long-held dream, because she had always longed to see the pyramids, the Nile and all the ancient wonders Egypt held.

She had loved her husband, Alex thought, watching as pain briefly darkened her eyes. Her voice held a thread of sadness when she mentioned her husband's name. Out of nowhere, he wondered how it would feel to be loved by such a woman.

Alex noticed that even John was listening, commenting on things now and then. How interesting, Alex thought, looking across at his friend and associate.

The stewardess came with the wine. Alex took it for her, chatting casually with the woman as he paid. Charmer, Jillian thought ruefully. She flushed, realizing that it was his charm that had led her to tell him so much about her life.

Her fingers trembled when she took the wineglass. "I'm sorry," she murmured. "I don't really like to fly."

Alex—he had introduced himself as Alex, but without telling her his last name—laughed and said that was the understatement of the year. He pointed out the window to the clear blue sky—an omen of good things to come, he said—then assured her that the airline had an excellent safety record. His friend, the older man with the haggard, world-weary face, eventually introduced himself as John. He joked and tried to reassure her, too, and eventually their efforts paid off. Once she felt a little calmer, she offered to move, so they could converse without her in the way.

Alex tightened his fingers around hers, and she felt the startling warmth in his eyes. His gaze was appreciative and sensual, without being insulting. She felt a rush of sweet heat swirl within her, and she realized with surprise that it

was excitement, that she was enjoying his company the way
a woman enjoyed the company of a man who attracted her.
She had thought she would never feel that way again.

"I wouldn't move for all the gold in ancient Egypt," he
said with a grin, "and I doubt that John would, either." He
touched her cheek. "I might lose track of you, and I don't
even know your name."

"Jillian," she said, meeting his eyes. "Jillian Jacoby."

He repeated her name softly, as if to commit it to memory, then went on to talk about Cairo, the pyramids at Giza,
the Valley of the Kings, and the beauty of the nights when
the sun set over the desert in a riot of blazing red.

And then the plane was landing. To her amazement, the
flight had ended. Once she was on solid ground again, Jillian realized that Alex knew all sorts of things about her,
while she didn't know a thing about him or John—not even
their full names.

They went through customs together. Jillian was immediately fascinated, in love with the colorful atmosphere of
Cairo, and not at all dismayed by the waiting and the bu-
reaucracy. When they finally reached the street she fell head
over heels in love with the exotic land. The heat shimmered
in the air, and taxi drivers in long burnooses lined up for
fares. She could hear the soft singsong of their language,
and she was thrilled to realize that the dream she had har-
bored for so long was finally coming true.

She didn't realize that two men had followed them from
the airport to the street. Alex, however, did. He saw the men
behind him, and his jaw tightened as he nodded to John to
stay put and hurried after Jillian.

"Where are you staying?" he asked her.

"The Hilton," she told him, pleased at his interest.
Maybe her dream was going to turn out to have some unexpected aspects.

He whistled for a taxi. Then, as the driver opened the door, Jillian looked up to find Alex staring at her. She felt...something. A fleeting magic raced along her spine, as if she knew what he was about to do. Knew, and should have protested, but couldn't.

Alex slipped his arm around her. One hand fell to her waist, the other cupped her nape, and he kissed her. His mouth was hot, his touch firm, persuasive. She was filled with heat; she trembled...and then she broke away at last, staring at him, the look in her eyes more eloquent than any words. Confused, she turned away and stepped into the taxi. As soon as she was seated she turned to stare after him, but he was already gone, a part of the crowd.

She touched her lips as the taxi sped toward the heart of the city. She shouldn't have allowed the kiss; she barely knew him. But she couldn't forget him.

She was still thinking about him when she reached the Hilton. She checked in quickly, but she was too late to acquire a guide for the day. The manager suggested that she stop by the Kahil bazaar, not far from the hotel. She dropped her bags in her room, then took another taxi to the bazaar. Once again she was enchanted. She loved everything: the noise, the people, the donkey carts that blocked the narrow streets, the shops with their beaded entryways and beautiful wares in silver and stone, copper and brass. Old men smoking water pipes sat on mats drinking tea, while younger men shouted out their wares from stalls and doorways. Jillian began walking slowly, trying to take it all in. She was occasionally jostled, but she kept her hand on her purse and sidestepped quickly. She was just congratulating herself on her competence when she was suddenly dragged into an alley by two Arabs swaddled in burnooses.

"What—" she gasped, but then her voice suddenly fled. The alley was empty and shadowed, and night was coming.

One man had a scar on his cheek, and held a long, curved knife; the other carried a switchblade.

"Where is it?" the first demanded.

"Where is what?" she asked frantically.

The one with the scar compressed his lips grimly. He set his knife against her cheek, then stroked the flat side down to her throat. She could feel the deadly coolness of the steel blade.

"Where is it? Tell me now!"

Her knees were trembling, and she tried to find the breath to speak. Suddenly she noticed a shadow emerging from the darkness behind her attackers. She gasped, stunned, as the man drew nearer. It was Alex.

Alex... silent, stealthy, his features taut and grim. Her heart seemed to stop. Had he come to her rescue? Or was he allied with her attackers, there to threaten, even destroy, her?

*   *   *   *   *

Watch for Chapter Two of SHADOWS ON THE NILE coming next month—only in Silhouette Intimate Moments.

Silhouette Intimate Moments

Starting in October...

SHADOWS ON THE NILE

by

Heather Graham Pozzessere

A romantic short story in six installments from best-selling author Heather Graham Pozzessere.

The first chapter of this intriguing romance will appear in all Silhouette titles published in October. The remaining five chapters will appear, one per month, in Silhouette Intimate Moments' titles for November through March '88.

Don't miss "*Shadows on the Nile*"—a special treat, coming to you in October. Only from Silhouette Books.

Be There!

IMSS-1

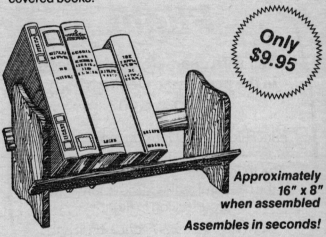

Silhouette Desire

COMING NEXT MONTH

#385 LADY BE GOOD—Jennifer Greene
To Clay, Liz was a lady in the true sense of the word, but she wanted more from him than adoration from afar—she wanted him to be this particular lady's man.

#386 PURE CHEMISTRY—Naomi Horton
Chemist Jill Benedict had no intention of ever seeing newsman Hunter Kincaid again. Hunter was bent on tracking her down and convincing her that they were an explosive combination.

#387 IN YOUR WILDEST DREAMS—Mary Alice Kirk
Caroline Forrester met Greg Lawton over an argument about a high school sex ed course. It didn't take long for them to learn that they had a thing or two to teach each other—about love!

#388 DOUBLE SOLITAIRE—Sara Chance
One look at Leigh Mason told Joshua Dancer that she was the woman for him. She might have been stubbornly nursing a broken heart, but Josh knew he'd win her love—hands down.

#389 A PRINCE OF A GUY—Kathleen Korbel
Down-to-earth Casey Phillips was a dead ringer for Princess Cassandra of Moritania. Dashing Prince Eric von Lieberhaven convinced her to impersonate the kidnapped heiress to the throne, but could she convince him he was her king of hearts?

#390 FALCON'S FLIGHT—Joan Hohl
Both Leslie Fairfield and Flint Falcon were gamblers at heart—but together they found that the stakes were higher than either had expected when the payoff was love. Featuring characters you've met in Joan Hohl's acclaimed trilogy for Desire.

AVAILABLE NOW

In response to last year's outstanding success, Silhouette Brings You:

Silhouette Christmas Stories 1987

Specially chosen for you in a delightful volume celebrating the holiday season, four original romantic stories written by four of your favorite Silhouette authors.

Dixie Browning—*Henry the Ninth*
Ginna Gray—*Season of Miracles*
Linda Howard—*Bluebird Winter*
Diana Palmer—*The Humbug Man*

Each of these bestselling authors will enchant you with their unforgettable stories, exuding the magic of Christmas and the wonder of falling in love.

A heartwarming Christmas gift during the holiday season...indulge yourself and give this book to a special friend!

Available November 1987

XM87-1